Thorvald has come

"What is it you want o   .
Although her mother ha   , Disa couldn't really
believe that this man standing before her intended to propose
marriage.

One blond brow lifted slightly. His voice rumbled low in
his throat, causing her heart to start drumming in an irregular pattern that spoke much of her trepidation.

"I only want what you are willing to give."

Surprised at the answer, Disa stared openmouthed. Only
what she was willing to give? Then he would get nothing
from her! Yet somehow, the words refused to come. Instead,
she ducked her head slightly to veil the hostility she was certain he could see in her eyes. She didn't know exactly what
deal her mother had struck with the giant, but she couldn't
bring herself to renounce it here by her mother's grave.

When Thorvald stepped closer, she jerked her head up, her
eyes going wide with consternation. He reached forth and
took one of her hands. Disa felt little prickles of ice run
along her nerves. She licked suddenly dry lips.

His eyes were empty of emotion, yet she could have sworn
she had seen sympathy there only moments before. "You
should have this," he told her, placing the cross in her palm
and closing her fingers around it.

She drew in a sharp breath at the familiar feel of the normally cold metal that had been warmed by the Norseman's
hand. Quick tears sprang to her eyes as she thought of what
this token represented. Her mother's last act of devotion.
Lifting her gaze to meet his once again, she gave an unconscious sigh.

He stared long into her eyes before he finally spoke. "When
you are ready, I will be waiting."

Turning, he left so quickly that she hadn't time to respond.

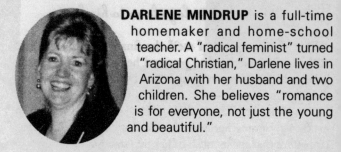

DARLENE MINDRUP is a full-time homemaker and home-school teacher. A "radical feminist" turned "radical Christian," Darlene lives in Arizona with her husband and two children. She believes "romance is for everyone, not just the young and beautiful."

Books by Darlene Mindrup

HEARTSONG PRESENTS
HP207—The Eagle and the Lamb
HP224—Edge of Destiny
HP243—The Rising Son
HP280—A Light Within
HP315—My Enemy, My Love
HP336—Drink from the Sky
HP376—Mark of Cain
HP419—Captive Heart
HP447—Viking Pride

Viking
Honor

Darlene Mindrup

Heartsong Presents

To Annette, Brenda, Christine, Colleen, and Yolanda, the fabulous five. Thanks for being my friends. I love you all. And to Jamie Beth, grandma's precious little girl. I love you, too.

A note from the Author:
I love to hear from my readers! You may correspond with me by writing:

Darlene Mindrup
Author Relations
PO Box 719
Uhrichsville, OH 44683

ISBN 1-58660-804-5

VIKING HONOR

Prologue

996 A.D.

The wind blew fiercely, pummeling the lone figure fighting her way up the rocky hillside. The old woman struggled against the almost hurricane-force winds, stopping periodically to catch her breath. She forced herself onward, fear lending strength to her weakening limbs.

A small hut rose before her, perched snugly within the sheltering confines of the hillside. Smoke drifted lazily from the opening in the thatched roof only to be snatched away almost instantly by the grasping wind.

Small, shuttered windows defied the zephyr's mighty power. Shaken angrily by the gusting and gyrating currents, they held firm. Like the man within.

The old woman hesitated briefly before taking her courage in hand and rapping firmly against the thick wooden portal. No one answered her summons. She lifted her fist again, banging louder, the sound almost drowned by the wailing wind.

Moments later, the door swung inward on well-oiled leather hinges. A tall, broad man stared out. His frosty blue eyes within his bearded face narrowed against the bone-chilling cold. Those eyes widened considerably on seeing the person who dared to intrude on his solitude.

"What do you want?" he growled, the wind no match for the timbre of his voice.

The old woman wrapped her cape tightly about her, as much to ward off the fear encroaching its insidious way up her spine as to ward off the falling temperatures. "I need to talk to you."

As the man moved to shut the door in her face, she stared at him fixedly, silently challenging him to let her have her say. He stood back and reluctantly motioned her in.

The door closed behind the woman, and she felt the first stirrings of real terror. No one knew much about this hulking giant, this Thorvald, save that he had been sent here to Greenland when he had been forced into exile from Iceland for murdering a man.

Yet he was her last chance.

The giant turned cold eyes upon her, one blond brow quirking upward. "You have a name?"

She met his eyes briefly. "Halgerd."

He bent to stir the fire in the middle of the room. Glancing quickly around, Halgerd was surprised to find the hut neat and tidy. This was somewhat reassuring, and she relaxed slightly. "May I sit?"

A touch of humor lighted the blue eyes. "Would it matter if I said no?"

Color flushed the wrinkled cheeks. "I would stand if you wish it."

Thorvald grunted, rising to his feet. He motioned to the bench behind her. "Sit if you wish, and tell me what is so urgent that it would bring an old crone like you out in such conditions."

Halgerd ignored the intended insult, lowering herself to the wooden bench. She joined her twisted fingers in her lap, her eyes resting on the gnarled digits.

Suddenly, she looked up and stared at him boldly, her courage rising with each passing moment. She was here for a purpose, and that purpose was a desperate one.

"You are Thorvald, late of Iceland?"

The giant's nostrils flared, his eyes growing colder than the North Sea. She studied his features through the hazy smoke drifting throughout the hut. The lamplight cast dark shadows upon his features, giving him a frightening appearance. His golden beard gleamed in the flickering flames of the fire. Though long in the way of the Viking, his hair was clean and well kept. Another good sign.

"I am," he agreed quietly. "Some call me Thorvald, the murderer."

Halgerd nodded. "Yes, I know."

His eyes flashed a look of irritation. "What is it you want with me, old woman?"

Taking a deep breath, Halgerd stated firmly, "I want you to marry my daughter."

❧

Thorvald caught his breath in astonishment. He stared at the woman as though she were some two-headed monster that had just crawled from the pit of the earth. He moved toward the door. "You need to leave, old woman."

His unwelcome guest did not budge. She pushed her black wool tunic against her legs in a nervous movement. Her faded gray eyes were serious with intent. "I am in earnest."

Thorvald was tempted to bodily remove the woman from his home, but in reality, he was just a little bit afraid. The woman was obviously mad, and there was no telling what a mad person was capable of doing.

Deciding to humor her, he crossed his arms over his chest and felt his soft leather shirt bunch against his muscles. "Go on," he said warily.

Halgerd took a deep breath. "My daughter, Disa, is in need of a husband. I think that you would suit."

Thorvald erupted in laughter. "You must be desperate."

Halgerd quickly looked away, but not before Thorvald had

seen the look in her eyes. He slowly unfolded his arms from his chest. "Is she that ugly then?"

Biting her lip, Halgerd shrugged. "It is not so much that she is ugly, as that she has a—a difficulty."

Thorvald sat down across from her, intrigued despite himself. Her notion of marriage was ludicrous; but having been scorned by his own people unjustly, he felt sympathy for the unknown girl. "And is this deformity so bad that no man will have her?"

Halgerd sighed softly, but he noted that she continued to meet his look steadily. "It is not a deformity of the body." She lapsed into silence.

Thorvald narrowed his eyes, his mind churning with unspoken questions. "I still do not see what this has to do with me. Where did you get the idea that I was looking for a wife?"

Looking around her slowly, Halgerd shrugged. "All men need a woman, whether they will admit it or not." She glanced at him and frowned.

"I have not done so badly caring for myself, old woman. What need have I of a wife? My animals keep me clothed and well fed; what more could I want?"

"Companionship." The one word, though lowly spoken, resounded through the quiet of the room.

Thorvald frowned. "I have no need of companionship. My animals keep me company enough."

Halgerd's voice became a little more desperate. "Disa could cook for you. Sew for you. I have taught her how to be a proper wife."

Thorvald sat back in his seat, eyeing Halgerd with some disquiet. "What exactly is the girl's problem that no man should want her?"

Color drained from the old woman's face. "When she was younger, she fell into the river. She was my only child. My husband and I could have no others."

She dropped her gaze to the floor, and Thorvald barely heard her softly spoken words. "Why is it that God favors some over others?"

Thorvald leaned forward, frowning. "God? Which god?"

Panicked gray eyes met Thorvald's curious blue ones. "No god. Any god," she answered cryptically.

Thorvald's unease grew by the minute. The old crone was obviously out of her mind. Still, the idea of marriage suddenly seemed not so ludicrous. She was right, though he hated to admit it. There were times when he thought he would go mad from the lack of human companionship. Although he had been forced into exile from Iceland, his solitude here in Greenland was by his own choice.

He looked across at Halgerd, the thoughts she put forth capturing his mind. He wondered why, just because the girl had fallen in the river, no man wanted her. He asked Halgerd.

The old woman fidgeted in her seat, pulling at her tattered wool dress. "She was dead when I found her," she stated quietly.

Thorvald felt his very blood turn to ice. Horror froze his heart. His throaty voice was raspy when he could finally get words past his lips. "You took her back from Hel?" How had the old woman managed to wrestle her daughter from the goddess of Niflheim? Dread filled his soul. What kind of power did this Halgerd possess?

The faded gray eyes sparked with anger. She met his look defiantly. "I do not believe that to be so. There must be some other explanation."

Thorvald stared at her, appalled. What other explanation could there be? Was the woman truly insane, or did what she say really happen? He slowly rose to his feet. "I think you should go, old woman."

Halgerd's shoulders slumped in defeat. A lone tear trickled down her wrinkled cheek. She glanced up at Thorvald's impatient clicking of his tongue. His gaze fastened on the tear sliding down her face.

"I am dying," she told him, holding her palms out in supplication. Her voice became choked with feeling. "When I am gone, Disa will have no one."

Thorvald turned away from her pleading face and threw more driftwood on the fire. Sparks scattered upward, while the wood sizzled and popped. He knew that he should just put the old woman outside and be done with it, but something held him back. His heart was wrenched with pity for Halgerd and this daughter of hers. He knew what it was like to be alone. He had two more years of exile before he would be free to return to Iceland. But did he really want to return?

He bit his lower lip. Yes, he wanted to. In two years, he could return to Iceland and restore the honor to his name. In two years, he would sail away from this inhospitable wilderness and return to a land even more desolate. When he did, it would be to track down the man who had forced him into exile.

He turned back to Halgerd, a sudden thought springing to mind. If he were married, he would seem less of a threat to the others, both here and in Iceland. The past might prove difficult for Disa to overcome while living in this settlement, but in Iceland, no one would know of her story. As for himself, having recovered from the initial shock, he wasn't too concerned about the idea of someone coming back from the dead. If that were so. Perhaps this Halgerd was making up a story to play on his sympathy. Whatever the reason, he was intrigued enough to consider her proposal.

He made his face carefully expressionless as Halgerd rose slowly to her feet. Haltingly, she made her way to the door. When she reached for the latch, Thorvald stopped her. "Hold."

She turned weary eyes on him.

"Your daughter, would she be willing for such a—an arrangement?"

An expression of joy flashed across her face and as quickly disappeared. "She is a dutiful daughter. She will abide by my decision."

Halgerd crossed to his side, removing a necklace as she approached. She handed him a silver cross exquisitely inlaid with stones of amber. Reluctantly, he reached out his hand and took it.

"When the time comes, give her this. She will know what it means."

He glanced at the cross suspiciously, then back to Halgerd. "I have not said that I agreed."

She shrugged. "The necklace is yours to keep, nonetheless."

Saying nothing, he curled the necklace into his large palm. "This is a cross," he stated. "A symbol of Christianity."

After a moment of silence, Halgerd answered quietly, "My family accepted Jesus Christ many years ago."

Thorvald wasn't surprised. He had encountered others who had turned from their traditional beliefs to worship this Jesus. Religion mattered little to him one way or another.

"I will think on what you have said," he told Halgerd, turning away with finality. He opened the door. The blistering wind came chasing into the room.

Halgerd ducked her head against the onslaught, passing Thorvald and giving him a brief look before she stumbled away from the cottage. She turned back for a moment, her straggled gray hair blowing about her face. Her voice could be heard above the keening wind. "I do not believe that you are a murderer, Thorvald of Iceland."

Nodding her head, she disappeared from view.

one

Greenland's spring was upon the land. Dark shadows dappled the sunlit grassy hills as puffy clouds skidded across the sky. A light breeze whispered across the land, adding a touch of coolness to the warmer temperatures.

Impervious to the signs of spring that bathed the landscape around her, Disa Halgerdsdottir stood silently beside the grave of her recently deceased mother. Her corn-colored hair flowed freely in the gentle breeze, her green eyes shadowed by the sadness and grief swelling through her.

Though it was the Viking way to lay stones in the form of an oval when burying their dead women, Disa had not done this for her mother. Instead, she had piled a mound of stones on top of the grave. Being Christian, neither she nor her mother believed in the Viking afterworld.

A raven cawed from high in the sky, his four-foot wingspan sending a speeding shadow across the ground. Disa shivered. Truth to tell, her faith was not as strong as her mother's had been, and she found herself suddenly questioning her belief in Jesus, the Christ. The raven was Odin's messenger, a harbinger of no good, of that she felt certain. She glanced at the sky but quickly turned away. She wouldn't give in to the doubts and fears unexpectedly assailing her.

Kneeling beside her mother's grave, Disa shoved a cross made of driftwood into the mound of stones. She stroked her fingers across the runes that spelled out her mother's name and sighed softly. She brushed halfheartedly at the tears winding their way down her white cheeks. Balling her hands into fists, she rose quickly; but her look stayed fixed upon the mound at her feet.

How long she stood thus, she was unaware; but suddenly, the hair rose on the back of her neck from a sure sense of someone's eyes studying her. Turning, she scanned the surrounding hills, her glance finally coming to rest on a giant Northman who stood watching her silently from some sixty paces away.

He slowly moved toward her, his frosty blue gaze never leaving her face. Various thoughts chased themselves through her mind at his appearance. Was he here like several others who had tried to wrest her land from her? If so, he was in for a surprise. She would not give up her land without a fight. It had been given to her father by Leif Eriksson himself to be held until the third generation, when it would revert to Leif again.

She knew what most of the people here thought of her. Word had spread that she had been to the netherworld and returned. They believed it was only a matter of time before the goddess Hel would demand she return to the world she had somehow been taken from.

Disa's mother had been feared by the people as a result of Disa's experience. Feared and hated. It was her mother who had breathed life back into her body, though no one knew how she had managed to do so. Halgerd was believed by most to be a witch.

Even those few who claimed Christianity had left the two women alone unless necessity forced them to do otherwise. Theirs had been a lonely existence, especially after Disa's father had died. Whispers abounded about his accidental death on a ship headed for the south. Whispers about Hel's revenge.

The stranger came to stand before Disa, his long blond hair whipping about from a sudden gust of wind. His cold, blue-eyed gaze penetrated the very depths of her soul. She drew in a quick breath, suddenly afraid.

"You are Disa Halgerdsdottir?" His deep voice reverberated off the craggy rocks around them. She had to look a long way up into his rugged face, her head coming well below his broad shoulders.

"I am."

Something in his look caused her heart to give an erratic thump before rushing on in an irregular pattern. Little tingles of apprehension shifted along her skin.

He held out a hand to her. Brows puckering with confusion, Disa watched as he opened his massive palm to reveal a piece of shining silver. A closer inspection showed it to be the cross her mother had worn every day until several weeks before her death, the preciously guarded relic having come with them through their travels from Norway.

The color drained from Disa's face, leaving her paler than before. She knew what that cross meant. After her mother had explained where she had taken the treasured item, Disa had spent days arguing with her about the unwelcome arrangement. Only her mother's death had put the debate permanently to rest. Disa slowly lifted her eyes until they met those of the man waiting patiently for her response.

Taking a deep breath, she pressed her lips tightly together to keep the volatile words waiting to be uttered from spilling forth. She struggled to calm herself before saying anything.

In the end, it was he who spoke first.

He briefly glanced at the rocky grave at her feet before looking beyond her to the icy waters of the fjord in the distance. "Niflheim cannot be much different from this place. Your mother should be comfortable."

His words meant to comfort did just the opposite. So long had she been raised in a Christian household that it was difficult to grasp what to her were the meaningless concepts of the Norse religion. The idea of her mother living in the frozen and misty Niflheim, home for the sick and old who died, held no appeal for her at all.

"My mother is not in Niflheim," she told him firmly. "She is in heaven."

His questioning look fixed on her once again. He looked down at the cross still clutched in his hand, and the perplexed look cleared from his face.

"Ah, I remember now. You are of the Christian faith."

There was something in the way he said the words that stiffened Disa's back. "What is it you want of me?" she finally managed to ask. Although her mother had prepared her, Disa couldn't really believe that this man standing before her intended to propose marriage.

One blond brow lifted slightly. His voice rumbled low in his throat, causing her heart to start drumming in an irregular pattern that spoke much of her trepidation.

"I only want what you are willing to give."

Surprised at the answer, Disa stared openmouthed. Only what she was willing to give? Then he would get nothing from her! Yet somehow, the words refused to come. Instead, she ducked her head slightly to veil the hostility she was certain he could see in her eyes. She didn't know exactly what deal her mother had struck with the giant, but she couldn't bring herself to renounce it here by her mother's grave.

When Thorvald stepped closer, she jerked her head up, her eyes going wide with consternation. He reached forth and took one of her hands. Disa felt little prickles of ice run along her nerves. She licked suddenly dry lips.

His eyes were empty of emotion, yet she could have sworn she had seen sympathy there only moments before. "You should have this," he told her, placing the cross in her palm and closing her fingers around it.

She drew in a sharp breath at the familiar feel of the normally cold metal that had been warmed by the Norseman's hand. Quick tears sprang to her eyes as she thought of what this token represented. Her mother's last act of devotion. Lifting her gaze to meet his once again, she gave an unconscious sigh.

He stared long into her eyes before he finally spoke. "When you are ready, I will be waiting."

Turning, he left so quickly that she hadn't time to respond.

Dropping to the ground, she buried her face in her palms and wept bitterly.

ða

Thorvald strode along the rocky terrain, his thoughts in turmoil. When the old woman Halgerd had come to his home months before, he had developed a less-than-flattering impression of her daughter's appearance; and Halgerd had done nothing to disabuse him of those notions during other visits she had paid to him before she died.

His first sight of Disa had shattered that preconception. Although not exactly pretty, Disa was definitely worth looking at. Her confident bearing would draw attention wherever she happened to go. She was no poor little creature who needed to be coddled. That had been plain to see by the fire in her eyes—eyes that reminded him of the dark green lichen that grew on the hills in Norway.

He had been drawn to her in a way that left him totally confused, although he wasn't certain why. When she had looked into his eyes, his mouth had gone suddenly dry, his heart rate accelerating to such an extent he thought it would burst from his chest. No woman had affected him that way in a very long time.

She, on the other hand, had seemed unaffected by their encounter. The only emotions he had seen in her eyes had been anger and fear. It pricked his pride that this would be so. Still, what did he expect? Even here, his reputation had been maligned. A murderer, they called him. He snorted softly. If only they knew.

He made his way down the sloping hillsides now covered with verdant green. Off in the distance, he could see the cattle and sheep from other farms contentedly grazing.

A frown twisted across his face. Too many people had become complacent with the warm temperatures and shorter winters they experienced in this settlement. They had refused to ready themselves last summer for a long winter; and when the winter had proven to be unusually cold with more snow than usual, they had run short on supplies. Many of their animals had starved to death. Some farmers had merely used the opportunity to feed their families with animals they knew could not survive, and now they lacked livestock to help them through the spring.

Thorvald had not had that problem. With nothing to do but work, he had filled his barns to the maximum with last summer's greenery. His own cattle and sheep had fared well, which brought him to another problem. The Manx sheep had started dropping their hefty fur, and he had no way to process it. A wife would certainly be a good thing to have right about now. Either that or a thrall who could spin and weave. His own clothes were becoming much too threadbare. Although he was good with a bow, knife, and spear, there were certain things that were beyond him. Like sewing clothing.

He hated the thought of purchasing a slave, but he could see no other way out of his dilemma. That is, unless Disa would consider adhering to her mother's promise. He supposed he could have pushed her, but standing by her mother's grave hadn't seemed the right place to do so.

Yet if Disa refused, he was going to have to either purchase a thrall or hire someone to process his wool. With that thought in mind, he headed his steps in the direction of Erik the Red's farm. Besides Disa, Erik was his closest neighbor. Since Erik had a number of thralls, perhaps he would hire one out to Thorvald.

He was halfway to his destination when he heard the horn blow, signaling an incoming ship. With the waters finally free from the ice pack of winter, more ships would be coming in. He quickened his steps, watching as the ship rounded the headland and came into view.

The knarr slid through the ice-dotted waters of the fjord and came to rest at the dock that had been prepared just for such ships. Several men scrambled over the side, making fast the vessel. One man stood off to the side, obviously the captain. Arms akimbo, he rattled off orders and watched as they were quickly obeyed.

It would take some time to unload the ship of supplies. Meanwhile people from the nearest farms gathered near the dock, soon forming a small crowd. More settlers would arrive in the next few hours from the surrounding vicinity, and later the trader would share his goods with still others by sailing to various fjords around the settlement that were too far to be reached on foot.

Eager faces waited for the ship to finish unloading. Thorvald noticed Eric limping toward the trader, his bristling red beard blowing in the wind.

"Ho, Erik!" the trader called.

Erik's face split into a returning grin. "Ho, Bjorn! It is good to see you again."

Both men slapped each other on the back, their lively voices fading as they turned away. Thorvald turned to watch the rest of the unloading. Although he had had very little business with Erik, those contacts had left an impression. When the hulking Viking had first heard Thorvald's story, he had smiled with sympathy and unabashedly welcomed

Thorvald to this paradise settlement that he had discovered. In the few times they had met since, Thorvald's respect for the man had grown considerably.

A lone woman rising from the bow of the ship caught Thorvald's attention. If she could be called a woman. She was thin to the point of boniness, her white face mottled by red welts. Her dark, lank hair hung dismally around her emaciated shoulders.

As she stepped forward, the sailors stepped quickly out of her way, averting their eyes as they did so. No one offered to give her a hand, and Thorvald grew intrigued. The girl must surely be a thrall. He stepped closer just in time to hear Bjorn telling Erik about the woman. "A raiding party gave her to me in exchange for some swords. They killed her brother, who happened to be a priest. She called down curses upon their heads; and although they laughed at her, it seems unusual things began to happen to them." He briefly glanced at the girl. "They wanted to kill her, but they were afraid. So they traded her to me instead."

Erik studied the girl with interest, as did the others standing around the ship. The girl stood with head bowed before them, and Thorvald felt his pity for her increase. He tried to shake off the feeling as a weakness, but it wouldn't be budged. She looked like a lost sheep expecting to be slaughtered at any moment.

"Were you not afraid of the curses yourself?" Erik asked, crossing the springy turf to get a better look at the woman.

Bjorn shrugged, following his friend. "I did not know about them until after we had sailed." He nodded at the girl. "She told me."

Surprised, Erik studied the girl more thoroughly. "She is English?"

"Aye, but she speaks Norse."

Thorvald noticed the trader shift uncomfortably before glancing back at Erik. "Perhaps you would like her for your own."

Apparently, Erik hadn't missed Bjorn's discomfort. His narrowed eyes focused on the trader. "What are you not telling me?"

Since Erik's hot temper was known throughout the Viking world and beyond, Thorvald thought the man would be wise to tread carefully. Honesty would definitely be the best policy.

"Well," Bjorn stammered, "unusual things have occurred whenever my men thought of taking the woman."

"Unusual?"

"Quick storms, breaching whales." Bjorn shrugged. "I would have killed her and thrown her to the sea gods, but when I was about to do so, we were suddenly beset upon by other raiders."

Obviously, Erik was not impressed with the trader's cowardice. Snorting, he made his way to where the girl stood leaning weakly against the side of the ship.

Curious, Thorvald moved closer to see what was about to transpire. Others nearby had heard the story and were whispering among themselves.

Thorvald hadn't noticed when Disa entered the clearing, but he recognized her standing on the fringe of the crowd. She watched the proceedings, her look focused on the strange girl. There was pity and sympathy in her gaze. It didn't take much to realize that she was probably feeling empathy with the girl, her own lot in life so similar.

Erik stepped closer to the side of the boat. "She looks diseased." He drew his sword from its baldric. "If you have not the courage to dispose of her, I will be glad to do it for you."

The whispers grew louder. Curses were not things to be taken lightly. The entire settlement could come to harm if the gods who were protecting the girl were angered.

"I will buy her from you." Disa's soft voice carried clearly to the men. Surprised, Thorvald watched her cross the clearing. Her gaze never wavered from the young woman in question.

Equally surprised, Erik and Bjorn watched Disa make her way forward. Bjorn's eyes took on an avaricious gleam. He bowed slightly to his possible customer.

"And what price would you be willing to pay?" he questioned, looking askance at the poor quality of her apparel.

"I will give you two silver coins," she told him, reaching into the bag fastened at her waist.

The trader hesitated. He searched the crowd to see if there might be a better offer. Although the crowd was still tittering with unease, no one challenged Disa's claim. The coins she had offered would buy one good cow—a fair price for a decimated thrall. When none came forth after several long moments, Bjorn sighed.

Disa motioned for the girl to come forward. The thrall struggled to get herself over the side of the ship and would have fallen, but Thorvald hastily stepped forward and caught her. Her eyes rounded with fear when they met his, and he could have laughed. There was no way on this earth that he would wish to take advantage of this haggard-looking thing who was being passed off as a woman. Still, having had his pity aroused, he set her gently on her feet.

When he glanced at Disa, he was surprised to see the look of respect she gave him. She placed two coins in the trader's massive paw, took the girl by the hand, and started to lead her away. Her eyes met Thorvald's one last time, then she turned her back on everyone.

The faces of the crowd watching Disa's departure were filled with animosity. Only one icy blue pair of eyes watched her with growing admiration.

two

Disa stood staring at the bright yellow-and-orange sky that reflected in the ice-dotted waters of the fjord. The fiery ball of the sun hung just above the horizon, creating the twilight that normally came just before sunset. Except here, the sun would set for only a few hours before it would rise to give them the many hours of daylight they needed to ready their farms once again for the long winter nights and days ahead. It would be months before they would see the long darkness again, but it would come eventually. Inevitably.

Only days before, the thought of that lonely, cold time had left her shivering with dread. Always before she had had her parents to keep her company through the long nights of winter. But no more.

Her face brightened slightly as she turned toward the house. Now it would be different. Now she had Agnes.

Opening the door, she entered the longhouse and made her way to the back, where the Englishwoman was huddled in a rapidly cooling tub of water. Agnes glanced up quickly when Disa joined her, her eyes full of the questions she didn't dare utter.

"This is a fine tub that your father had made for you," she said instead, giving a tentative smile.

Disa returned her smile in full. Avoiding the puddles of water soaking into the earthen floor, she seated herself on a stool, allowing her fingers to glide over the fine workmanship of the wooden tub. Father's friend Regis had built it in exchange for several of Father's fine Manx sheep. Being a shipbuilder, Regis had built the tub in the clinker style of the long ships that so gracefully sailed the sea. It had been a sacrifice of precious wood, but Regis had wanted to get married and he'd needed some animals to start his farm. Although most tubs were used simply to create steam in a family farm's steam house, Disa had always loved the sensation of immersing her body into warm water.

Disa studied Agnes, noticing how the water had taken away the grime and revealed a truly lovely young woman. Only the red dots on her face marred its perfection, and those would fade in a short time now that they had rid Agnes of her body lice. It was fortunate that the young woman didn't have the head lice that were so much more difficult to eradicate.

Agnes's hair hung long down her back, its dark color made even blacker by the wetness from its severe washing. She lifted brown eyes still filled with sadness and loss, and Disa's heart went out to her once again.

"Tell me about yourself," Disa requested, shifting slightly on the wooden stool to make herself more comfortable. Although the girl seemed to have lost some of her earlier terror since Disa had shared her own faith in Christ, it was obvious that she was still afraid.

Agnes ducked her head, lifting the precious bar of soap that Disa had given her to use. The soap had been purchased especially for her mother on one of her father's trading expeditions. He had brought back two bars of the lavender-scented soap, knowing her mother's penchant for cleanliness. He had teased her mother about it often, but he had been proud of his wife—even though he had considered her a little eccentric at times. This bar was the only one that remained, and it would be hard to replace since the traders who came to this island were more concerned with carrying the goods so needed here. Still, Disa had been happy to share her precious hoard with Agnes.

"What is there to tell?" the girl asked.

Recognizing she was about to cause Agnes great pain, Disa still persisted. "Tell me about your brother."

The flash of grief was quickly veiled by the dark eyes that turned Disa's way. "He was a priest."

Disa tipped her head slightly in acknowledgment. She already knew that from the conversation by the ship. "Were you close to one another?"

Agnes smiled dreamily, nodding her head. "We were very close. Never would I have imagined that the brash, teasing boy of my youth would one day long to be God's servant. He was a horror when we were children, always into mischief."

Disa leaned closer and handed Agnes the towel that she had heating by the fire. Having been an only child, she envied the girl. Impatient to know more, she pleaded, "Go on."

Agnes took the linen towel and, rising from the water, began to briskly dry herself. Waiting for further instructions, she wrapped the sheet around her, shivering with the cold.

Disa quickly got up from her stool. "Let us get you settled before you continue your story, though I have to admit, I am anxious to hear more." She smiled, and the tense look on Agnes's face eased.

"You have been very kind to me, my lady," she stated quietly.

Shaking her head, Disa laid a hand on Agnes's arm. "I am not 'my lady' to you," she told her firmly, determined to disabuse her of the notion that she was a slave. "I am just Disa. At the next Althing, I will proclaim you free, and that will be the end of it. In the meantime, I give you your freedom. I do not need a slave. I need a friend."

Her softly spoken words brought a quick look of relief to the other girl's face. Disa handed her one of her own linen kirtles. "You can wear this for the night. On the morrow, we can start to make you some clothes. I had to burn your others."

Agnes wrinkled her nose, giving an elfin quality to her face. "They were not worth saving, I am afraid, but they were all that I had."

Disa returned to the front of the house to give the girl some privacy. Typical of other homes in the settlement, her house had several rooms: a kitchen room, a great room for eating and sleeping, a pantry or storage area, and an area where animals were kept. She began to arrange food on the table for their evening meal. Having been gone most of the day, she had not had time to prepare some bread, but the stew would be welcome without it.

Agnes finally joined her. "Is there anything you wish me to do?"

Disa motioned her to a place at the table. After they both sat, Disa handed Agnes a bowl of stew. "Please, I would like to hear more about your brother."

Hesitating, Agnes glanced at the stew, then at Disa. "My brother taught me to always give thanks to the Lord for my food."

Surprised, Disa jerked back her hand that had been reaching for the spoon. Although her parents had claimed Christianity long ago, neither knew much about the way the religion was practiced. Feeling the heat warm her cheeks, Disa wondered if she had been offending the great God of heaven all of this time.

Slowly, Agnes reached out to take Disa's hand and bowed her head. Just as slowly, Disa followed suit, keeping her eyes on the other girl.

"Father, we thank You for the food You have set before us. And thank You that You have brought me to safety and have set my feet before a friend. In my Lord Jesus' name, amen."

Letting go of Disa's hand, she lifted her head. Agnes's simple prayer stirred a yearning in Disa that surprised her. Was it possible for just anyone to speak to God that way? Was it not blasphemous to do so? Once again, Disa reached for her spoon, though her appetite had suddenly diminished.

Agnes took up her own spoon, the firelight glinting off of the hammered silver. Her face took on that faraway look that Disa had noticed earlier.

"My brother heard a priest read the Scriptures one day when we were at mass. He said that something about the words stirred his heart; and from that time on, he wanted only to study the Scriptures. Since only the priests have such knowledge, he decided to become one. He went to Rome to study."

Tears came to Agnes's eyes, and Disa wasn't certain if it was due to the girl's painful memories or the thickness of the smoke from the fire in the room. The small hole in the thatched roof designed to allow the smoke to escape was far from adequate.

"I remember when he came home, how bright his face was. He was so full of God's Word that it seemed to spill from him."

Awed, Disa sat quietly, her food forgotten. What must it be like to know the very words of God? "And did he teach you?"

Agnes grinned impishly. "From sunrise to sunset. He was forever making me repeat verses from Scripture after him." The smile suddenly fled. "It was those very words that gave me some measure of peace over the last few weeks."

The pain in Agnes's words reached Disa. They were alike in many ways, this Englishwoman and herself. Both had suffered loss. Both had suffered rejection.

"Tell me why the others saw you as cursed."

Taking a deep breath, Agnes pressed her lips tightly together. When she exhaled, she drooped forward with discouragement. "I have repented of my words, but they had a lasting effect." She pushed her bowl away.

The silence in the room seemed to go on forever before Agnes finally broke it. "I was visiting my brother at the monastery when the Vikings came. My brother took up arms to defend me."

Disa's eyes widened in surprise. "A priest?"

A half-smile formed on Agnes's lips. "Although my brother became a priest, that was only so that he could study the Word of God. I do not think that he really had the heart of a holy man." She smiled with pride. "Like King David in the Scriptures, he held too much of the warrior in his soul."

Noticing Agnes shiver, Disa rose from her seat. "Let us sit closer to the fire."

They both settled near the flickering flames, the snapping and popping of the peat the only sound disturbing the stillness. Disa handed Agnes a comb, and she began to slowly work the tangles from her clean hair. Her voice took on a singsong quality that mesmerized Disa. As Agnes's story progressed, the dark shadows at the perimeter of the fire seemed to come alive with menacing movement. Disa shook her head to rid it of such fanciful thoughts.

"I believe it was my brother's courage that caused the Vikings to spare my life. The other priests threatened them with crosses. My brother took down four of them with his sword before he was finally slain."

The sentence ended on a whisper. Disa reached across and gently squeezed the young girl's hand in sympathy. Agnes turned to Disa, and her beautiful brown eyes were dark with unspoken memories.

"One warrior raised his sword to strike me down. I remember screaming at him that just as he had slain my brother, God would strike him down." She stopped, staring somberly into the flames. "I must have spoken in Norse, because he was so startled that he stopped with his arm raised. I saw the look of fierce anger on his face replaced by one of sheer surprise. Seconds later, he fell at my side with my brother's knife sticking from his back."

"Your brother was not dead?" Disa asked hoarsely.

Agnes shook her head, staring back at Disa sadly. "He died only seconds later," she breathed softly. "Another warrior who had witnessed the whole thing decided to take me with him instead of killing me."

"Then what happened?" Disa asked, wanting to hear the rest but suddenly afraid to.

"The first several days at sea, we were wracked by storms. I heard the sailors complaining that they had never seen anything like it. Then, when the storms subsided, the men had time to think of other things." She grew suddenly still.

"And?" Disa prompted.

Agnes bit one corner of her lip. "I–I remember being lifted to my feet. The men were laughing. The man who was holding me tried to kiss me." Tears of shame sprang to her eyes before she continued. "I begged them to let me go, but they only kept laughing. I do not remember much else except that there was a strong lurch of the ship and most of the men were knocked from their feet. I remember falling to the deck when the man holding me released me to try and gain his balance. I did not see it happen, but the others said that a whale breached right beside us, knocking the man into the sea. I do not know what happened after that, but he never resurfaced."

Disa's eyes grew wide with wonder. She slowly let out the breath that she had been holding. "Surely God was watching out for you."

Agnes smiled, but the sadness never left her eyes. "They thought me cursed after that and refused to have anything to do with me. They wanted to throw me over the ship, but

I saw the terror in each man's eyes. They feared that something would happen to them if they did me any harm."

Knowing Viking valor as she did, Disa was not surprised that they would be afraid of the woman. Even seasoned warriors feared the gods.

Seeing Agnes's eyelids drooping with fatigue, Disa got to her feet and pulled a fur pelt from the pile on the earthen bench that ran along the wall. "You can sleep there," she told Agnes. "In the morning, we will discuss what we will do."

Agnes thankfully took the pelt and lay down on the bench. Disa sank to the matching bench that ran along the opposite wall, and after some time, Agnes's even breathing filled the room.

Disa lay wide awake, her thoughts running in circles. Had she done right by saving the girl? Was the girl protected by God Himself, or was she truly cursed? She supposed only time would tell. Remembering Agnes's petition at the meal, Disa felt again the wonder of talking to the great God of the universe. Closing her eyes, she hesitantly tried to do the same thing.

&

Disa awakened to the sound of thunder. She blinked sleepily before realizing that the sound wasn't coming from the sky, but from her own door.

Agnes huddled against the wall, a look of stark terror on her face. Smiling reassuringly, Disa hastily pulled on her tunic, attaching the apron overdress at the shoulders with her favorite brooches.

The pounding came again just as she reached for the handle, causing her to jump slightly. Growing aggravated, she flung the portal wide.

Horik Rifgurdsson stood before her, his look of impatience growing to match Disa's. The beard on his face ruffled slightly with the breeze of a new morning, but the look on his face was not friendly.

Disa wondered what had brought the man to see her so early in the morning. His farm lay some distance away to her right, his property adjoining hers.

"I wish to talk to you," he told her peremptorily.

Disa lifted one brow at the arrogance of his tone but reined in her impatience. She had learned long ago that Horik had thoughts for no one but himself, and it did little good to remind him of his manners, for he hadn't any.

"What do you wish to speak with me about?" she asked him, not bothering to invite him inside. Recognizing the snub, his face grew stormy with the temper for which he was so famous.

"I want your land."

Surprise rendered Disa speechless. Taking her lack of words for agreement, he went on.

"Since your land adjoins mine, I would like to use it to graze my cattle and sheep."

His look passed over her slowly, and Disa didn't like the gleam that came to his eyes. "I will pay you for the house and barns."

Recovering from her shock, Disa glared at the man before her. Crossing her arms over her chest, she asked him, "And just what am I supposed to do?"

His insulting look passed over her again. "Find yourself a man." He grinned slowly, and Disa knew a sudden apprehension. "In fact," the man sneered, "I have a son who needs a wife."

"This land is mine," Disa ground out, "and it will stay mine!" She thought it best not to tell the man that she wouldn't marry one of his sons if he were handed to her on a silver platter.

Horik's eyes narrowed. "You are a woman alone. You cannot take care of this land. It will only go to waste, and I have need of it."

"Your needs mean nothing to me," Disa choked out, her cheeks flaming with her own rising temper. "Be gone from here, Horik. You may have neither my land nor my home."

Reaching out, he lifted her by her upper arms until her eyes were level with his own. "Do not try my patience, Woman, or you might learn more about a man's needs than you could handle."

Disa admitted to herself that the man did intimidate her. He had a reputation as a wife beater, and she knew his threat was not idle. He was the only man who had ever seemed to lack any fear of her. Stifling her panic, she told him in a firm voice, "Get your hands off from me!"

A slow smirk lifted one side of his mouth as he took stock of her petite frame. "Perhaps you would like to make me," he growled savagely.

"Perhaps I would," a male voice answered, coming from behind Horik.

Startled, Disa and Horik turned to see Thorvald standing a few feet away. His immense size and blazing eyes started Disa's heart drumming with fear. Horik must have felt much the same way for his grip slackened. Taking advantage of the moment, Disa stepped out of his reach.

"What business is this of yours, Thorvald?" Horik called out, his voice filled with anger.

Thorvald caught Disa's look before answering. She couldn't miss the warning in his eyes.

"The woman belongs to me."

Two pair of eyes rounded in surprise. Disa wanted to deny the charge, but thought better of it. Thorvald's warning had been clear. Even Horik held Thorvald in great esteem, though he was obviously jealous of him. It would take a better man than Horik—or a drunken fool—to challenge someone like Thorvald. Right now, Horik was neither.

Horik looked suspiciously from Thorvald to Disa. Finally, he shrugged his shoulders in seeming indifference. "I did not know. Then it is you I should be asking about the land. Since your land is farther inland, you cannot farm the two. I will give you a fair price."

Thorvald's voice rang with a certainty that was not to be gainsaid. "The land belongs to Disa. It was given to her father by Leif, and it is hers until it passes on. . . ." He paused, then continued to speak with deliberation. "Until it passes on to our children."

Disa could not have begun to describe the feeling that washed over her at his words—a curious mixture of fear, shock, and anticipation all rolled into one. She wasn't certain which man had taken the greater leave of his senses.

"We shall see," Horik argued vehemently. "Leif gave the land to Olaf and his sons. Not his daughters."

Thorvald lifted a brow in question, looking at Disa for confirmation.

"That is not true," she denied angrily. "Leif gave it to my father for two generations, at which time he thought to return and make his home here."

Horik stepped toward her, his brow furrowed in anger. A slight movement from Thorvald checked him. He glanced at Thorvald, and an uneasy look crossed his face as he noted Thorvald's hand resting easily on the sword in its baldric.

"If there is a dispute," Thorvald told him calmly, "it will be decided at the next Althing."

Horik's hands curled into fists at his side. "I have not the time for that. I need this land to graze my sheep and cattle."

Thorvald merely continued to stare at him until, with an

oath, the other man turned away. The look Horvik threw Disa before he left promised retribution, and she had to hold back the shiver that threatened to betray her feelings.

She bit her lip, wrapping her arms around her waist defensively. With a feeling of dread, she watched Horik stride down the hill. It took her some time to get her feelings under control before she could finally turn to face Thorvald.

"I thank you for what you did," she told him, "but there is one thing you need to know here and now. I do not belong to you."

Unperturbed, he smiled back at her, making her grind her teeth together with frustration.

"We shall see," he told her, his blue eyes crinkled with laughter.

three

Thorvald watched the door close behind Disa's retreating back, and a sudden grin split his face. He hadn't the vaguest idea what had possessed him to tease her in such a way, but he had a feeling it had something to do with the dent she had made in his pride.

The grin left his face as suddenly as it had come when he remembered the sight of Horik gripping Disa by the arms and dangling her above the ground. Such rage had filled him at the man's temerity that he had nearly succumbed to the desire to draw his sword and slay Horik where he stood. Only exerting powerful discipline over his thoughts had enabled him to keep his calm.

So Horik wanted Disa's land. That might just work in his favor. Horik's presence in the situation might make her a little more malleable, and Thorvald wasn't above pressing a point when it was necessary.

Stepping forward, he rapped on the firmly closed portal. At first, he thought Disa was going to ignore his summons, because he was certain that she knew it was he. After some seconds had passed though, she pulled the door slightly open and quirked an inquiring brow at him.

"I did come for a reason," he told her, careful to keep the laughter out of his voice.

She gave him a suspicious look. "And that is?"

He frowned impatiently. "Might I come in and discuss it with you?"

She hesitated a moment before standing back and motioning

him inside with obvious reluctance.

Thorvald ducked his head to miss the low doorframe, allowing his eyes to adjust to the darkened interior. He noticed Disa's thrall huddled in the corner of the bench that ran along one side of the room. His surprise must have shown on his face, for the corners of Disa's lips lifted in an impish smile.

"This is Agnes."

Although still thin to the point of boniness, the young woman had changed from a filthy urchin into quite a lovely young woman. Thorvald allowed his gaze to slide over her, noting her almost flawless features despite the thinness of her body. He felt a stirring of interest that quickly passed when he turned back to Disa.

"I came to suggest a bargain," he said, carefully studying Disa's reaction.

Various emotions crossed her face before she finally looked at him with mistrust. "What kind of bargain?"

Thorvald looked pointedly at the bench behind him. Disa followed his gaze. Sighing, she shrugged her shoulders. "Would you like to sit down?"

Without answering, Thorvald seated himself, allowing space for Disa to sit next to him. Instead, she chose to sit next to Agnes, the table spanning the space between them. The two women watched him, their suspicions evident. Feeling his irritation rising, Thorvald frowned at both of them. "I have need of someone who can spin and weave. I thought that if you would be willing to do so, I would, in turn, take your goats and cattle up into the hill pastures for you each day and return them for milking that evening. I would also cut the grass and store it in your barns for the winter."

Disa bit her lip in indecision. Only that morning she had been wondering how she was going to be able to make Agnes a tunic and still drive her animals up into the hills. Although

Agnes could weave the material herself, the task would go much more quickly if they worked together, and the girl needed something to wear quickly. The thin kirtle would not protect her from the chilly winds that blew across the land. What Thorvald suggested would answer her needs, as well as his own. Yet, she was reluctant to get involved with him in any way.

He shrugged. "It was only a suggestion. Horik would then have no cause to bring complaint against you for allowing the fields to go fallow."

The thought of her morning visitor brought Disa up short. The next meeting of the Althing was only weeks away, and she knew with certainty that Horik would be bringing a case against her at the assembly of lawgivers.

Surely Erik would listen to her since it was his son Leif who had rented the land to her father. But if she didn't show her ability to bring in the hay and take care of the land, Erik just might side with Horik.

"That would be agreeable to me," she finally told Thorvald, her voice filled with the discomfort he engendered in her.

His steady regard brought the hot color to her cheeks, but she found herself unable to look away from him.

He nodded slightly, finally releasing her from the spell he seemed to wield over her. "Then I will start today. Come show me what all needs to be done, and I will do it."

Disa ignored the hand he held out to her and walked past him to the door. Being near him unsettled her in ways she had never thought possible. Although he was behind her, she could feel his exasperated gaze on her.

She took him to the barns, and together they toured the buildings, discussing what needed to be done. His intelligent suggestions surprised her. But what did she know about him, really? He was a recluse, an outlaw, and a murderer. But her instincts had never failed her where people were concerned;

and her instincts told her, against all reason, that she could trust this man. At least to a point.

She suddenly realized that he had stopped talking. Turning, she found him studying her in puzzlement.

"I asked if you would like me to bring my wool to add to yours?"

She blushed, realizing that she had been daydreaming about him. "That would be fine. Agnes and I will start carding our wool immediately after we have eaten."

He looked as though he were about to say something. Instead, he nodded slightly and, turning, strode quickly away.

Disa watched his disappearing back. He was a man of fine stature; that was for certain. Even Agnes had been enthralled by the man's appearance. And although Disa was used to seeing the same icy blue eyes among her people, his held something that strangely intrigued her.

Agnes joined her, a fur pelt wrapped around her kirtle. She followed the direction of Disa's gaze. "He is quite a man, is he not?"

Disa pulled her thoughts together and turned to the other woman. "We shall see," she told Agnes, remembering that he had spoken the same words only moments before. Only in a far different context. Little butterflies danced around in her stomach at the thought of what his words had implied. She had a strong suspicion that, one way or another, Thorvald would have his way in the end.

"Come, Agnes. We must get busy and make you a dress."

They spent little time on their meager meal, both anxious to start carding so that they would have enough wool to weave a dress. From the looks of Thorvald's clothes, it wouldn't be long before he would need a pair of trousers also.

As Agnes carded, Disa spun the wool onto spools. Spinning was backbreaking work since it required her to stand on her feet all day; and by the end of the afternoon, Disa had a headache brewing from constantly bending forward as the spool spun to the floor.

After awhile, Agnes came and took the distaff from her shoulder. "Here, let me spin for awhile. You can sit and card."

Relieved, Disa didn't argue. Sitting down and curling her feet under her, she started vigorously scraping the brushes together.

"Tell me more about the Scriptures, Agnes. What kind of things do they talk about?"

Agnes reached down to curl the spun yarn around the spool, then set the spool spinning again. "Well, they tell us how we ought to live."

Frowning, Disa allowed the brushes to go lax in her lap. "In what way?"

That started Agnes on a discourse of the Scriptures that lasted the rest of the evening. Disa lost awareness of the time as she sat riveted, hearing for the first time the Word of God. Time seemed to fly by on wings; and before Disa realized it, she could hear Thorvald returning with the goats.

Hastily getting up, she hurried to open the door and saw Thorvald's back disappearing around to the back of the house where she kept her animal pens. She glanced over her shoulder at Agnes. "I will return in a moment."

She shut the door behind her and hastened after Thorvald. As she approached, he looked up from latching the gate.

"Everything is well?" she asked, not really certain why she had followed him.

He gave her an affirmative nod as he continued tying the leather strap that held the gate closed. He glanced at her in question. "Did you expect otherwise?"

How was she to answer? If she told him no, he would wonder why she had followed him out here. If she told him yes, she would be lying. She chose instead to change the subject. "I thought perhaps you might like to share the evening meal with Agnes and me."

He straightened slowly, turning to study her. Retrieving the stick he had used to drive the herds to pasture, he told her softly, "I think not tonight. There is still much I have to do at my farm."

For the first time, Disa realized just how much work helping her would entail. There would be far more work on his side than hers. The bargain was slightly off balance.

She laid a hand on his arm and felt the shock of it all the way down to her toes. His eyes quickly met hers, and she knew that he had felt it, too.

"I—I just wanted you to know that. . .that Agnes and I will be ready to start carding your wool as soon as you bring it," she stammered out in a rush.

The pupils of his eyes had darkened so much that his eyes looked black. He moved closer, and Disa took a hasty step in retreat. A fire seemed to ignite behind his eyes. He took a deep breath and turned away. "I will bring some of my wool when I return in the morning. There is no hurry for you to process it, though. Do your own first."

Disa knew that she would only work as much of her wool as was necessary to make Agnes a dress. The rest would have to wait until she had completed her part of the bargain. Her father and mother both had taught her the importance of fulfilling a contract. It was a matter of honor; and, though the people in the settlement may not have held her in much esteem, she held herself to her own rigid standard.

She watched Thorvald leave with mixed emotions. What had made her ask him to share their meal in the first place? Her feelings about the man were ambivalent, to say the least.

She made her way back to the house, stopping at the door

to stare out over the fjord. The calm sea reminded her of a jewel her father had shown her from far away. The green gem had glistened in the light, much like the fjord reflecting the light from the waning sun.

Feeling the need for some exercise after being shut inside for most of the day, she called to ask Agnes if she would like to join her for a walk. Disa gave her her own kapa to wear over her kirtle. The long cloak was lined with fox fur and would keep the girl warm as well as modest.

They both ambled down the rock-strewn hill to walk along the waters of the fjord. The bay was still dotted with the chunks of ice that broke from the moving glaciers that flowed over the countryside and down to the sea. As the summer progressed, the ice would continue to melt until eventually the fjord would be free of it.

Disa and Agnes walked some distance, finally coming out on the shores where the ice that broke off from the frozen ice pack farther north made its way before melting in the warmer waters. It was here that everyone came to collect driftwood for the fires and other odd tools that required the much-prized wood. The low-lying scrub trees that grew on the land offered little useful wood, and most of the larger trees had already been felled.

Disa described to Agnes her life in Greenland, remembering fondly her father and mother and recalling the happy times they had had together.

"You loved them very much." It was more a statement than a question.

Disa nodded, swallowing hard. Her grief was still fresh, and it didn't take much to bring her near to tears. She turned to the other woman.

"You may find it hard to believe, Agnes, but I believe that you were sent here by God Himself."

Surprisingly, Agnes agreed. "I did not understand how God could allow the things to happen that He did, but I think that I do now. Although I could wish it had never happened, I know that my brother is with the Lord, so I do not need to worry on his behalf."

Seeing the desperate sadness in Agnes's brown eyes, Disa realized something for the first time. The two shared one more thing: a deep grief.

Twilight was over the land again. Since it would not grow completely dark for some time, Disa didn't worry about the distance they had traversed. When the skylights appeared, they would provide enough light to get home. The shifting patterns of colored light still thrilled her no matter how many times she experienced them. There was something so unearthly about them that it gave rise to strange beliefs even in her own mind. Deciding it would be wise to turn back, Disa led Agnes toward home.

Suddenly, the girl stopped, staring out over the water. "What is that?" she asked.

Disa followed the direction of her gaze but could see nothing in the dim light. "Where? I do not see anything."

Pointing, Agnes told her, "There. On that chunk of ice floating just over there."

Straining her eyes, Disa finally made out a small, dark object on the piece of ice that Agnes had noticed.

"I cannot tell what it is. Perhaps it is something of worth that we could use. Often things are brought to us with the tide."

Agnes shook her head slightly. "It looks like some kind of animal."

As the ice floated closer, Disa could see that it was indeed a small animal. "Whatever it is, it seems to be dead. If we could get to it, we might be able to collect its fur and use it."

She wrinkled her nose slightly. "But it would depend on how long it has been dead."

She tried to decide if it would be worth the effort. Although her father had left her mother well supplied with silver and other goods, it had been almost two years since his death, and they had had to use their money sparingly since. It was fortunate that the sheep kept her well supplied with wool, Greenland wool being in high demand back in Europe because of its soft texture. The cows had also helped to supplement their income with the cheese that was so popular over the seas as well.

The money was beginning to run out, however, since she had not had enough in trade goods to purchase everything that they had needed. Iron for the tools was a precious commodity and cost a great deal of silver. And since her mother had refused to own thralls, the extra work of bringing in the hay had been almost impossible.

Disa began chewing on her bottom lip, a nervous habit she had developed long ago. "I do not know how to get to it. I have no boat."

Agnes slanted her a peculiar look. "Perhaps Thorvald would help."

Disa glanced up the sloping hill behind her. They had come almost to Thorvald's farm, and it was possible that he just might be willing to help them. Her face set stubbornly, then just as quickly relaxed into acquiescence. There really was no other way that she could think of. And though one fur was not much, a fur was still a fur.

She tried to see Thorvald's house but knew that it lay hidden behind the hills. He had always preferred living alone and did not welcome visitors. It had taken great courage for her mother to approach him.

Thinking of her mother decided the matter. Lips pressed

together, Disa told Agnes, "Wait here."

As she climbed the hill, it occurred to her how her mother must have felt those months ago when she had trekked up this ridge to face a man accused of murder and ask him to marry her only daughter. For a moment, she stopped, pressing her hands against her suddenly hot cheeks; but thoughts of her mother's courage forced her on.

Thorvald's house came into view, dark against the surrounding silhouettes. Smoke drifted from the hole in the thatched roof that hung low to the ground. What must it be like to shut oneself off from everyone else and live so alone? She felt a strong surge of pity for his loneliness, though she doubted he would welcome her pity. He was far too self-sufficient to need it.

The closer she got to the house, the more her heart began to pound. She felt no fear, only an odd sense of expectancy.

She rapped strongly on the door. It was opened almost immediately, and Disa took a hasty step back when faced with Thorvald's heavy frown. Recognizing her, his frown increased.

"What are you doing here?"

She clutched her hands behind her back, twisting them nervously. The wind blew much fiercer here, and Disa brushed impatiently at the tendrils of hair clinging to her face.

"I—I have come to ask a favor."

His eyebrows rose slightly. He folded his arms over his massive chest, a slow smile spreading across his face.

Disa swallowed hard, realizing that he knew full well the effect he had on her.

"Indeed?"

Her courage almost failed her. What was there about this man that could so instantly fire her desire to be contrary? She couldn't look him in the face, afraid of what she might see.

Turning, she motioned the way she had come.

"Agnes and I were out walking when we noticed something floating on the ice. We think it may be an animal, and we thought we could retrieve it for the fur, only we do not have a boat to get out to it and—"

He stopped her prattle by touching her arm. She jerked her gaze back to his face and was not surprised to see him laughing.

"Do not make such hard work of asking a favor," he told her, the grin never leaving his face. "Wait here a moment."

He ducked back into the house, reappearing with a walrus-hide rope flung over his shoulder. Taking her arm, he pulled her along.

"Come. Show me where."

They made their way back to where Agnes stood waiting, her attention still fixed on the piece of ice. She pointed it out to Thorvald.

"You are lucky," Thorvald told them. "My boat is just behind that ridge."

The women followed him to where his small craft used for fishing lay nestled safely among the rocks. He lifted it easily from its resting place, holding the small boat over his head. The muscles in his arms bulged against the weight, and Disa felt herself shiver. It seemed possible that Thorvald had the power to kill a man with his bare hands. She wondered again what the story was behind his outlawry. For all his strength, there was a surprising gentleness about him.

Thorvald settled the craft in the water. "I will need one of you to come with me. You will have to hold the boat steady while I retrieve whatever is on the ice." Agnes and Disa exchanged glances. Agnes's eyes told Disa that there was no way she was getting into a boat voluntarily with such a giant. Sighing, Disa moved past the waiting Thorvald and gingerly climbed into the boat.

❧

Trying to hide the smile playing about his lips, Thorvald watched Disa settle herself. He wasn't sure if she was truly afraid of him or if it was something much more basic. At her farm earlier, he had been affected by her simple touch; and when he had searched her eyes, he had seen his feelings reflected there. He could feel the strong attraction between them. It had been there from the beginning, surprising him with its intensity. But Disa was fighting it all the way.

He stroked evenly with the oars, keeping an eye out for floating ice. He allowed his look to rest on Disa. She was certainly no beauty, but something about her had attracted him from the start. It was becoming increasingly difficult to turn his thoughts away from her.

The oars dipped steadily through the calm waters. As they neared the ice, the object on it began to take shape. Thorvald recognized that it was an animal of some sort—a rather small animal, perhaps a fox.

They carefully drew up beside the ice, and Thorvald had Disa take the oars and hold the boat steady while he attached a line to the ice. The ice was too small to hold his weight, so he used his hooked rod to catch the creature by the fur and pull it toward him, careful not to damage the fur.

He lifted the animal into the boat and caught a surprised breath. It was a young wolf pup, obviously starved. He wondered where it had come from. In all of his expeditions to the north part of Greenland, he had never seen a wolf pup. There were beautiful white bears, plenty of foxes, and the reindeer his people hunted back home; but he had never once seen a wolf.

Disa took the pup, while Thorvald released the line from the ice. When he turned back to face her, she was holding the pup close against her chest, her beautiful green eyes wide with surprise.

"It is alive, Thorvald."

His mouth dropped open slightly. He certainly hadn't expected that. Moving closer, he ran his hands over the animal, feeling its bones through its fur. The poor creature must have been on that ice for some time.

The pup never opened its eyes to acknowledge their presence. It was obviously close to death, most probably from starvation. He pulled a knife from its sheath, and Disa's eyes grew wider.

"What are you going to do?"

He motioned to the pup. "It is dying. Better to make it quick. And although it is still a pup, you will be able to use its fur."

Her eyes flashed at him, and she began shaking her head slowly. "No. You cannot kill it."

He frowned as he reached for the animal, but Disa pulled away from him.

"I can try to save him. He would be good company for Agnes and me."

Beginning to doubt the woman's sanity, Thorvald relaxed against his seat. He could tell by the look in her eyes that there would be no gainsaying her. He wanted to reach out and snatch the wolf from her arms, quickly dispatching it before she could stop him; but the consequences of the action stopped him. Disa was just beginning to trust him. She had shown that by coming to him for help. He couldn't take a chance of disrupting that growing faith in him.

He shrugged, but his anger simmered just under the surface. If the woman was fool enough to take a near-dead animal and try to make a pet of it, especially a wolf, so be it. It was nothing to do with him

"As you wish, but do not come to me when the animal becomes so weak he has to be put out of his misery. The job is yours."

four

More than a week passed before Disa had a chance to go to Brattahlid, where the trader had been staying. Word had come to her that Bjorn had finished his business among the various fjords of the settlement and that he would be leaving that day. Disa desperately needed some things, and she hoped that she hadn't left it too late.

When she passed through Erik's farm on her way to the dock, she noticed people staring at her, then quickly turning away. Several chattering women looked at her with open envy. Listening to bits of conversation as she passed, Disa realized word that she was Thorvald's woman had spread. Hot color burned in her cheeks, and she hurried her steps onward, pulling her sledge over the rocky ground.

Bjorn stood watching his men load the ship, giving orders when needed. His rust-colored hair hung long down his back, his bright red tunic making him stand out from the others. She wondered if the color choice was deliberate so that no one would be able to miss his presence.

Erik joined him near the shore. Although the people in Greenland had chosen to model their law after the Althing in Iceland, there was no denying that being the founder of the colony gave Erik a stronger voice. Evidence of his advancing years was apparent; but there were few, if any, who would dare to challenge the man's authority.

The two men were deep in discussion when Disa reached their location. She heard Erik inviting Bjorn to join them for the spring festival that would soon begin. People would be making their way from all over Eriksfjord to join in the celebration of the arrival of the warm sunshine once again flowing over the land.

Disa felt her insides go cold at the thought. She hated the pagan rites that so many indulged in. There would be heavy drinking and carousing and offerings of sacrifices to the gods. She decided to make her purchases quickly and retire to her home.

The trader glanced up as she approached, a slow smile lifting his lips. If not for the carved lines on his face from heavy dissipation, he would have been considered a fine specimen of manhood. His bloused trousers ruffled in the strong breeze, making him appear even larger than before. His brow rose in inquiry.

"Well, if it is not the woman who would take on the gods. If you wish for the return of your money, I am afraid that is not possible."

"I have no wish for my money back," Disa returned haughtily, knowing he referred to Agnes and her supposed curse. "I have come to trade with you for some needed items."

He held his hands out to his sides, smiling apologetically. "I have very few goods left, I am afraid. Almost everything that I brought has been taken."

Her heart sank. "I have need of an iron pot."

He shook his head. "My apologies, but the ones that I had have been purchased."

Disa's heart sank further. She knew that she should have come earlier, but between caring for the wolf pup and trying to get Agnes's dress made, she had had very little spare time. She brushed a hand down her own worn tunic, wondering how she would be able to make do without the items she needed. Her only iron pot had cracked when the support for it had broken loose from the roof and the pot had crashed onto the rock beneath it.

"Have you any wooden buckets?"

Shifting from one foot to the other, Bjorn again shook his head apologetically.

Disa sighed. Now what was she to do?

"Perhaps you would care to take a look and see if there is anything that you need among my supplies," the trader suggested, motioning to the few bundles still left to be loaded onto the ship.

Disa nodded slightly. "I will do so. Thank you."

He allowed access to his goods while continuing his conversation with Erik. As she searched among the supplies, she became aware of Erik's intent perusal. She tried to ignore him while at the same time she couldn't help but hear the conversation between the two men.

"Although it was you who brought the mead," Erik laughed at Bjorn, "we would be willing to share it."

Disa sighed. Greenland didn't possess a bee population to produce honey necessary for making the alcoholic drink. If there were mead to be had, some of the men might make a celebration of the event and later run wild. She would do well to get her things and return home as quickly as possible.

She covertly studied Erik and wondered if the accident he'd had before Leif left on his journey had made him look older than she had ever seen him. Erik had planned to lead that expedition himself; but when his horse had thrown him and injured his foot, he had deemed it a bad omen and changed his mind. Leif had been given charge instead.

"Well, did you find anything?"

Startled, Disa glanced up to find Bjorn watching her. She smiled.

"Yes, actually, I did," she told him, lifting a few items from the packs spread out before her. "I could use some of these bone needles and a basket or two."

He bowed low before her. "Whatever my lady wishes."

Disa pulled forth her sledge, still loaded with bags of eider down. "Here are my trade goods." She knew that two bags of eider down were not much to bargain with, but it should be more than enough for what she had chosen

Bjorn opened the bags, shoving his hands deep into the sacks. A sudden gleam filled his eyes, and he smiled slowly.

"A fair trade," he told her.

"I also have need of a pair of dress brooches."

Bjorn crossed his arms over his chest, pursing his lips in consideration.

"Hmm, I do have some brooches, but they are rather costly. I am afraid that your down would not be enough to purchase them and the other items."

Disa waited while the trader opened a chest and removed several pairs of brooches. All were exquisitely wrought of the finest silver and inlaid with pieces of amber. Disa caught her breath at their glowing beauty.

"They are lovely," she whispered, awed by their perfection. She had thought Bjorn might be trying to trick her into purchasing something that had little worth; but as she examined the brooches, she knew he had spoken the truth when he'd said that they were worth more than the down she had with her. She smiled sorrowfully at the trader, handing back the brooches. "I cannot afford what these must surely cost."

Erik took one of the brooches and turned it in his hands. He looked at Disa for a long minute, then turned to Bjorn. "Give them to her. I will recompense you."

Both turned astonished looks on the older man. Disa opened her mouth to protest, but Erik lifted a hand to stop her. "I owe Thorvald. This is my gift to you."

It was well known that Erik had a fond place in his heart

for Thorvald. Some thought perhaps it was because he and Erik's younger son shared the same name. Personally, Disa thought the relationship had more to do with the fact that both men seemed to have similar personalities. Regardless of the reason, she needed to disabuse him of the notion he had formed about their relationship.

Disa shook her head, ready to deny everything. Her eyes burned with anger; but before she could speak, Bjorn handed her the brooches.

"I did not know that she was Thorvald's woman." He smiled at her, and Disa was amazed at the amount of respect she was suddenly accorded. How could a man who was considered an outlaw for murder engender more honor from his colleagues than herself, a woman who had done nothing to anyone? And how was she to set the matter straight about her not belonging to Thorvald? The bargain she and Thorvald had made was beginning to take on alarming significance.

The situation was fast slipping out of Disa's control. She opened her mouth again to deny everything, then thought better of it. It would never do to put such a slur upon Thorvald's honor, although he more than deserved it since he was the one who had claimed to Horik that she belonged to him. Besides, Erik probably wouldn't believe her anyway.

Reluctantly, she took the brooches and added them to the needles and baskets. She thanked Erik politely, though she thought the words would surely choke her.

She waited while Bjorn had his men unload her sledge of the bags of feathers, then she hurried home with Erik's words still ringing in her ears.

When she reached her farm, she unwillingly exchanged the brooches on her dress for the ones Erik had given her. She silently handed her old brooches to Agnes. If it hadn't been that Agnes needed the brooches in the first place, none of this would have happened. Disa sighed. No, she couldn't blame Agnes. The woman had not asked for anything; it had been Disa's idea to surprise her new friend. She glanced down at the bright silver shining from the front of her own dress and felt marked somehow.

Agnes turned Disa's old brooches over in her hand as she followed Disa into the kitchen area of the sod house. "You should not give me these. They are your favorites. You told me so yourself."

Disa bent over the pallet where the wolf pup lay sleeping. For a week, both she and Agnes had taken turns spooning goat's milk and broth into the creature's mouth. He had at least recovered enough so that now he could manage to eat the broth on his own.

Thorvald had not been pleased. He'd told her that the pup was at least four months old, and that, someday, he would turn into the killer he was meant to be.

Disa didn't believe him. She stroked the pup's fur, marveling again that he could have survived on the sea. How he had gotten there in the first place would probably always be a mystery. Thorvald had suggested that perhaps he had come from the land to the west that Leif was now exploring.

She placed the bone needles on a shelf. Having already told Agnes what had transpired at Brattahlid, she smiled at the girl's refusal of the brooches.

"I could not refuse Erik's gift," Disa explained. "It would have been an insult. And I cannot wear two pairs of brooches at the same time." She smiled slightly. "Besides, you had need of them; and though I would gladly give you these that I now wear, I cannot."

Agnes nodded. "I understand."

Disa grabbed some food to eat on her journey, took one of the baskets that she had traded for earlier that morning, and went to the door. "I am going to check on my eider duck nests. It will take me some time, so do not be alarmed if I do not return until late."

"I will go with you."

Disa shook her head. "No, there is still much to do here. We should be able to finish your dress tonight, then we can start on Thorvald's wool. I will be all right."

She opened the door, ducking out into the sunlight and allowing her eyes to adjust from the darkness of the interior. "The trader said that he would return before fall. We will have to start stocking our trade goods. When the sloeberries ripen, we can use them to dye some of our wool. That will give it added value. In the meantime, continue to spin the wool that we have on hand. Thorvald will need his for trade also."

Disa closed the door behind her and wondered if Agnes would be all right staying alone. She had no fear for herself, for no one had ever dared to bother her. She wrinkled her nose slightly. No one, that is, except Horik.

The day was warm, and the bright sun hung high in the sky. The scent of the sea breeze blew in from the fjord. For the first time in a long while, Disa felt content. She still grieved for her mother, often finding herself wishing to share some item with her the way they always had, but she was content nonetheless. That was in big part due to Agnes's presence. They had formed a strong bond of love in such a short time that Disa was amazed that it should be so.

Several hours of climbing and walking passed before she reached the eider duck nests that were nestled among the rocky hillsides. All of the nests she claimed as her own were filled with feathers and eggs. She decided to add a few more nests by placing rocks in such a way that the eider ducks would see them as natural nesting spots. The next time she came, they should be full.

She shooed off the nesting birds. After that she went around to the full nests, removing the eider down and the duck eggs and placing them carefully into the basket she had brought with her. Although she hated to take the eggs, they were considered a delicacy by her people and would bring her some profit. The main profit, however, would come from the down that was so popular in Europe. The ducks would strip themselves of their own feathers to layer their nests for their eggs. This made it easy to retrieve the down without injuring any birds.

Disa would return in several months to do the same thing again. The poor ducks were either very stupid or very stubborn. After the eggs and down were removed, the ducks would try again to start a nest in the same location. She would be able to remove the down several more times before the end of the season, when she would leave the last eggs to hatch for next year.

The hours passed, and the sun started to fall in the sky, telling Disa that, although it would be hours before darkness, she would be wise to start for home. Realizing that she was hungry, she decided to eat the rest of the bread that she had brought with her before making the long return trip. She set down the basket, twisting her shoulders back to relieve the ache that had been forming for some time.

Taking the loaf from her pouch, she sat down and leaned back against the rocks, enjoying the sunshine and the day. A feeling of euphoria settled over her. She lifted her face to the azure sky and, without thought, began thanking God for being with her and taking care of her.

Since Agnes had come into her life with her knowledge of the Scriptures, Disa had learned that the great God of heaven wanted a personal relationship with her. He wanted to be her Father, not just her God. Having lost both of her beloved parents, this was a comforting thought that warmed her as nothing had before. Always before she had feared the Christian God; but now she knew that, although He was to be respected and worshiped, He wanted above all to be loved. How it must pain Him to be rejected by so many of His children. She could understand that better than anyone.

Her thoughts drifting, she failed to notice the fog that slid stealthily over the land. The weather on Greenland was volatile, changing rapidly at any hour. She should have remembered.

Getting to her feet, she quickly started back to the farm, hoping to outdistance the creeping mist; but the cold fog thickened around her, hindering her progress. She wasn't alarmed; but if the fog lasted, she could find herself tumbling down some rock face and injuring herself.

Finally, the fog became so thick that she lost her bearings. She stood still, biting her lip in indecision. What should she do? She couldn't stay out all night because, even though sunset would occur hours from now, the air would grow colder as the sun dipped toward the horizon, and she could freeze to death. She had already begun to feel the temperature drop before the fog came, and now the moisture had intensified the cold.

She turned slowly in place, not able to see more than a foot beyond her. Crying birds in the distance lent an unearthly sound that was swallowed up by the ever-thickening fog. Stepping back, she felt the ground give way beneath her. Arms flailing madly, she did what she had feared most and tumbled down a bank to land with a thud against the rocky ground.

She lay still for a few seconds, trying to catch her breath. Her ankle throbbed. Stars seemed to swim alarmingly before her eyes. When she tried to sit up, her stomach and sides burned with pain.

Moaning, she managed to pull herself into an upright position, flinching against the pain. When she gingerly tried to stand, she cried out in agony and dropped back to the ground. Her ankle pounded with excruciating pain, making the bile rise in her throat. She would be unable to stand.

Sore and bruised, she stretched her injured leg out before her while drawing the other leg up against her chest. Resting her face against her knee, she began to petition the Lord softly. A lone tear slid down her cold cheek. "Help me, Lord. Oh, please, help me."

෨

Thorvald brought the goats and cows down from the pastures later than usual. The day had been warm, and he had decided to allow the animals more time to graze before bringing them back home to milk.

When he had noticed the fog drifting in, he had hurried them back to their shelter. Although the fog might disappear as quickly as it came, he didn't want to chance losing an animal in the thick mist. After closing the fence behind him, he took the time to check each animal, making certain that they were free from diseases and other pests. He rubbed a hand over the thick fur of the goats, noting that it would soon be time to bear their young. The sheep in the pastures were also ready to lamb, and Disa would have quite a herd if all the ewes produced healthy offspring.

He checked the barns to see how much space he would have for hay. The buildings were quite large, although they were almost empty. Disa's father had done well in building this farm, even though he knew that it would one day return to Leif. Probably the deal had been that given the land for his use, Disa's father would receive a large payment from Leif if it had been managed well. It was no wonder that Horik had set his greedy eyes on the place.

Since the barns were empty of hay, Thorvald wondered how Disa had thought to survive the winter. Even with Agnes, there was no way the two women could have managed. The thought brought a dark frown to his face.

After he had completed his tasks, he was in no hurry to leave. The fog had grown thicker, and no pressing needs drove him to leave for his own farm. He had very few animals to tend, preferring to make his living hunting.

He settled down inside the dark barn to wait out the weather. Although he had no doubts of his ability to find his way home, the silence of his house held little appeal.

Stretching his long legs out before him, Thorvald pulled a piece of hay from the dwindling stack and began to chew on it thoughtfully. Lately, he found himself increasingly reluctant to leave Disa's farm and return to his own.

Often, while he tended to things in the barns, he heard Disa's and Agnes's laughter. In such a short time, the two had become firm friends. He envied that.

Most people left him alone because they thought he wanted it that way, and in the beginning, that had been true. But lately, he found himself yearning for company—the kind of companionship that Disa and Agnes seemed to share.

The barn door creaked open on its leather hinges, and Agnes hesitantly stepped inside. Surprised, Thorvald got quickly to his feet, brushing the hay from his clothing.

"Thorvald?"

Her hesitant voice came to him through the darkness, and he realized she couldn't see him in the dim light of the enclosure.

"I am here," he told her, stepping forward.

She came closer, leaving the door open behind her to give her more light. When her eyes adjusted to the dark, she quickly came to where he stood. "I am concerned for Disa," she told him without preamble.

His stomach gave an uncomfortable lurch. "She is not well?"

"She is not here. She went to the eider duck nests late this morning and hasn't returned." Her brown eyes were alive with worry. "She told me not to be concerned if she did not return for many hours, but with the fog. . ." She left the words hanging.

Thorvald's lips pressed tightly together, his nostrils flaring. Leave it to Disa to go off by herself. There was no telling what might happen to the woman in this fog. He smiled reassuringly at Agnes, though he was far from being reassured himself.

"I am certain she is well. I will go look for her."

Alarmed, Agnes grabbed his sleeve. "The fog is too thick. You will do yourself an injury. Besides, how will you see?"

He began gathering his things together. "I will use my sunstone to guide me. As long as I keep on a path to the north, I will be all right."

Agnes followed him outside, and he walked with her to the door of the house. When she turned to him again, doubt covered her face, but all she said was, "Take care."

He nodded, waiting until she shut the door behind her. He trotted up the hill toward his house as rapidly as he dared in the soupy mist. With his inherent sense of direction, he had no trouble finding his house.

He went straight to the chest in the corner of the room and rummaged through until he found what he was looking for. The sunstone was one of his most prized possessions. The amber stone helped him see through the fog and find the sun because it turned dark blue when pointed north.

Adding the sunstone to his pouch, he then searched until he found some clean rags to use in case Disa was injured. That thought left him slightly queasy.

The more he thought about it, the angrier he became. The foolish woman! She needed someone to look out for her; and since he had given his word, he guessed that honor, such as it was, belonged to him.

He made his way down to the shore. Turning the sunstone slowly, he determined the location for true north. He followed the coastline in a northerly direction for some time, marking the trail as he went so that he could easily find his way back. The eider nests were many miles from the farms; and fortunately, he didn't have to contend with darkness, although the fog was problem enough. Besides, darkness would come soon. He had to find Disa and find her quickly.

It took him much longer than normal to reach his destination. When he got close to the nesting grounds, he started making his way inland and began to shout. The fog distorted the sound, making him realize that if Disa did manage to answer him, it would probably take some time to find her. His anxiety grew, and with it, his temper escalated.

There was no answer for some time, so he continued searching until finally a quavering shout rewarded him.

Listening carefully, he followed the sound of Disa's voice until he came upon her sitting in a slight cleft. She huddled, shivering against the creeping chilly air, tear stains dried on her cheeks. The feeling of relief that swept over him was palpable.

He cautiously slid down the hill to land beside her, stones skittering in his path. "Are you all right?"

She nodded her head slightly, her chin quivering with emotion. "I have hurt my ankle. I do not think that I can walk."

The relief he felt was quickly swamped by a flood of anger, "What were you about, Woman? Have you lost all reason?"

She glanced up at him, her mouth open to reply, when she suddenly burst into tears. He knelt beside her in an instant. He wasn't quite certain what to do, never having been able to deal with a woman's weeping.

"I thought that I would have to stay here all night," she sniffed.

Swallowing his ire, Thorvald lifted her gently into his arms. Their gazes held; and seeing the pain shimmering out to him from the green depths of her eyes, Thorvald felt his remaining anger slide away.

"You are the most vexing woman," he told her in exasperation.

He stood and shifted her weight into his arms more firmly. She nestled against his chest, and his next words dried up in his throat. He no longer felt the cold. Instead, he was slowly being flooded by a warmth he was quite unprepared for.

"Why did you come for me if you think I am so vexing?" she asked, her own irritation evident in her voice.

Thorvald studied her face for a long instant, trying to reconcile in his mind the childish voice he was hearing with the woman's body he held in his arms. Part of him wanted to cuddle her as if she were the child she was behaving like. Another part of him responded to the woman she was. He finally swallowed hard and told her, "You belong to me, Disa. I always take care of what is mine."

He knew that was the wrong thing to say as soon as the words left his mouth.

❧

Disa's eyes blazed with the heat of her wrath, her mouth parted with surprise. "You. . .you. . ." Bereft of words, she stared at him in impotent rage. What could she say in the face of such arrogance? "I never said that I would marry you!"

He glared back at her indignantly. "It went without saying. Your mother said it for you."

When she spoke, her voice was several times its normal volume. "I do not wish to marry you!"

Thorvald stopped in his tracks, his own anger more than a

match for hers. "You would dishonor your mother?"

Disa retreated into silence. Only that morning, Agnes had shared a Bible verse with her that spoke of honoring one's parents. Her eyes met Thorvald's with silent appeal. "I cannot marry you."

He opened his mouth to say something, then snapped it shut. He began striding back to the farm, paying little heed to his steps.

"Wait! My basket!"

Blazing eyes met hers, and she closed her mouth on further words. "I will retrieve your belongings later," he told her inflexibly.

Disa watched his set face without appearing to do so. That he was in a towering rage was all too apparent.

The silence between them lengthened. Finally, Thorvald stopped to rest. He settled Disa on a rock and went to sit some distance away. He avoided her gaze and, instead, stared morosely into the surrounding mist.

Disa missed the warmth of his body and soon began to shiver with the cold. If he noticed, he gave no indication. She tried to tell herself that it didn't matter, but she wasn't fooling herself. It had felt so right to be held in his arms. She had felt protected. Comforted. Truth to tell, she had wanted to stay there much longer. Her reasons for refusing to marry him had grown cloudy in her mind, much like the thick fog around them.

Her shivering increased, but still he paid no attention. How long would he continue to stand there moping? Growing aggravated, she clumsily tried to get to her feet.

He glanced hastily her way, a quick frown forming on his face. "What do you think you are doing?"

"I am going home," she told him, her voice shaking despite her attempts to keep it firm.

His lips thinned with displeasure. "How?"

Disa lifted her chin, glaring coldly at him. "I will crawl if I have to. You need not concern yourself with me further."

His long sigh spoke clearly of his aggravation. "Your gratitude leaves much to be desired."

His words made Disa pause. What he said was true. Thorvald could have been killed coming in such a fog to look for her. The thought chilled her more thoroughly than the cold. And if he hadn't come for her, she would probably have died from exposure.

Though instantly contrite, Disa still had a hard time saying the words she knew she needed to say. "I beg pardon. You are right, I have been truly ungrateful."

His face relaxed, and he came and lifted her back into his arms. His gaze met hers.

"Thank you for coming for me," she said so softly that he bent nearer to hear.

His look rested on her trembling lips before returning to her face. "You will marry me, Disa," he told her, his throaty voice instantly unsettling what little composure she had managed to find. "It is inevitable."

Disa could find no words to say. The brooding intensity of his look left her more uncertain than before. She had the sinking feeling that an immutable force had been set into motion, a force over which she had no control.

five

It wasn't very hard for Disa to avoid Thorvald for the next few weeks. He was extremely busy taking care of the livestock, and she was trying to heal from her accident.

For the first few days, Disa lay in bed while Agnes attended to the chores, although Agnes was hard put to keep Disa from getting up and attending to her own duties. After Disa healed to a point where she could move without excruciating pain, she was at least able to finish weaving the cloth to make Agnes's dress. Using the last of the saffron that her father had brought back from one of his travels, they had dyed the wool a beautiful yellow.

With the new clothes, clean body, and proper nourishment, Agnes became not only lovely but truly beautiful. It was no wonder the raiders had chosen her, though to their obvious regret later on.

One thing became clear to Disa: Agnes was truly protected by the great God of heaven. Disa never tired of listening to her recite Scriptures, and Agnes never seemed to tire of saying them. She exuded such peace that it was a joy just to be around her.

It would seem that Thorvald felt the same way. Disa noticed his eyes wander Agnes's way quite often when he thought no one was looking. It caused Disa a pang that she refused to give a name to.

She studied her own worn and frayed garment and decided that perhaps when she had the time, she should make herself a new one also. But for the moment, that would have to wait.

Too many preparations for winter remained to be made, and summer in Greenland was over much too quickly.

Like most of the neighboring farms, Disa's farm produced cheese, butter, and wool for trade goods. It would soon be time to start the cheesemaking, but in the meantime, she started working on the butter.

Thorvald offered fish and reindeer that the two women couldn't supply for themselves in exchange for the butter that he had neither the time nor the resources to make. Disa couldn't help noticing just how well they worked together. She had to admit that having Thorvald around certainly made life a lot less complicated, and she was fairly certain that he felt the same about her. She tried to decide if that thought pleased her or not.

The Althing would meet in a few weeks, and Disa was a little concerned about how the other Greenlanders would feel about Agnes being in their midst. Truth to tell, Disa herself had never attended the Althing, though her father had. Both Disa and her mother had felt it wiser to remain at home.

Disa had heard the stories of celebrations that had taken place during other Althings. It was a time of camaraderie as well as for law. So often Disa had wished that she could go and participate. When she was younger, she had even dreamed about meeting a man who would wish to marry her. In her thoughts, the man always loved her. She had never contemplated an arranged marriage.

Agnes joined her in the kitchen. "Thorvald brought more fish," she said, laying them on the table. "Should we pickle them, salt them, or dry them?"

Disa checked her barrel of salt and noticed that it was lower than she would have wished. "Let us dry them this time. We should probably save the salt for the cheese."

Together they deboned the fish. Agnes sliced it into thin

strips, while Disa laid the strips out to dry.

Agnes peeped at Disa from the corner of her eyes. "Thorvald is a fine man, is he not?"

Disa felt again that strange pang. She continued to carefully lay out the strips, but for some strange reason, her hands started shaking. She took a towel and began wiping her hands, forcing a smile. "In what way?"

Agnes shrugged, her cheeks blooming with soft color. "I mean that unlike the rest of your people. . ." The English-woman stopped, looking suddenly contrite. "My apologies, Disa. I did not mean. . ." She stumbled into silence.

Disa cupped Agnes's chin in one hand, lifting her face until they could look each other in the eyes. "It is all right, Agnes. I know the reputation of my people; and while they have done much to create that impression, many of my people have chosen a different way, a more gentle way."

Agnes's look grew intense. "You mean because of the Lord Jesus Christ? Is Thorvald then a believer?"

Back to Thorvald again. Was the girl smitten with the hulking Norseman? The thought left Disa unsettled. She would hate to see Agnes get hurt. She firmly pushed aside any other thoughts about why she might not wish to see them together.

"I do not know Thorvald's beliefs, but I do not believe he is a believer of the Lord."

Agnes's face fell. "I thought. . ."

Again she left the words hanging. Disa picked up the bowl with the fish entrails and heads. Setting it outside the door for Thorvald to dispose of later, she turned back to Agnes and firmly put an end to the discussion of her erstwhile suitor. "I think you must ask Thorvald if you want to know his beliefs."

❧

Thorvald brought the goats down early, peeking his head in the door to let them know. "There are some things that

I must attend to at my farm."

He noticed Disa staring disconsolately at the iron cauldron sitting in the middle of the wooden table.

"Is something wrong?"

Disa sighed, motioning to the pot. "It is the only iron pot I have that is large enough to make the cheese. Without it, the process will take much longer."

Thorvald came fully into the room. "Is something wrong with the pot?"

Running her finger along the crack that extended halfway down the side, she told him, "It is cracked, and I have not the skill to repair it."

Thorvald lifted the heavy cauldron into his hands as though it were a mere feather. He turned it until he could see the crack better, then glanced up at Disa. "I should be able to fix this. Do you need it today?"

Relieved, Disa gave him one of her best smiles. His reaction was a slight narrowing of the eyes. She hastened to assure him, "It can wait until tomorrow since you have things to attend to today. Can you really fix it?"

It was not that she doubted his expertise, but iron was hard to come by, and extra iron would be needed to fix the crack. She wondered how he would manage.

He looked at her with calm assurance. "I will bring it back to you tomorrow." When he reached the door, he stopped. Taking a deep breath, he turned back to her, his assurance suddenly gone. "I wondered. . ."

Disa was surprised by his reticence. He was so ill at ease that it made her reluctant to know what was on his mind. Twisting her hands behind her back, she asked hesitantly, "Yes?"

He pressed his lips tightly together an instant, then rushed into speech as though he needed to say it fast to get it out.

"I wondered if you might be willing to put up some cheese

for me also. I know it is hot, hard work; but it brings much more in trade goods, and I haven't had time to do as much hunting."

The reason he didn't have as much time to hunt was obviously because he was spending so much time helping Agnes and herself. Disa smiled at him. "We would be happy to do so, Thorvald."

When his gaze met hers, some unnamed emotion lurked in their frosty depths. Her heart increased its rhythm tenfold. She took a steadying breath and turned away. "We have been thankful for all the work you have done for us. We could not have done it without you."

Realizing what she had just said, she whirled back to face him, her eyes wide with consternation. She met his cocky smile with a frown, but he refrained from commenting on what she had said. Still, it was there in his eyes. *I told you so. You need me!*

Her words could not be unsaid. She pressed her lips together tightly. "Do not let me keep you," she told him breathlessly. "I know that you have much to do."

His smile broadened slowly, and Disa wanted to shake him. Her gaze traveled over his broad form, and she swallowed hard. It would take someone with much greater strength than she to do so.

He lifted the pot slightly. "Tomorrow," he said.

The door closed behind him, and Disa sank onto a bench. Agnes eyed her shrewdly.

"Yes," she intoned softly. "A fine man."

❧

It was a fine day for the Althing to meet. The sun shone brightly from a blue sky with a soft wind blowing. People had been gathering at the meeting place for some time, many coming from several miles away. There were also those who came by boat, choosing the quicker way to travel the miles across the fjord.

Children scampered about, their laughter ringing on the clear morning air. Women chatted in gossiping groups, happy to have companionship with those they hadn't seen in some time.

Disa was not one of the chattering group. She stood to the side with Agnes, her gaze wandering over the gathering throng. Agnes's eyes shone with excitement. Today would be her day of freedom, but Disa wasn't altogether certain that that was all that was causing the feverish glitter in her friend's eyes. Perhaps Agnes was unaware, but Disa had noticed several men eyeing the beauty with open admiration, some with open lust. Disa grew tense. She hoped there would be no trouble, although the mead that had been saved for the occasion was flowing freely.

Erik sat as head godi among the chosen group of other godar. Although they were called priests, in reality they served merely as judges. They busily consulted with one another, their fierce frowns making Disa suddenly afraid.

A cool hand settled on her arm, and she turned to find Agnes watching her sympathetically.

"It will be all right, Disa. God is with us."

Disa remembered Agnes quoting something from God's Word that talked about Jesus being the Prince of Peace. Scripture also said Jesus told His disciples that He was leaving His peace with them. She only had to remember that Jesus was always near and that He would never forsake her. She felt the strength returning to her shaking limbs.

Together the two women walked around the large group of people. Everywhere people mingled together, not only visiting with each other, but also trading with one another. Since she had never been to the law assembly before, no one from the farther distances recognized her. Only those who lived close by eyed her with open hostility.

Before long, Disa noticed that increasing numbers of people were turning to watch her progress. Word was spreading rapidly among the group.

Agnes sidled closer, taking a firm grip on her hand.

Disa felt someone watching and turned to find Horik standing close to Erik, his intent gaze watching her every movement. She shuddered at the coldness of his eyes.

Pulling Agnes along, Disa hurried away from the area. There would be time enough to face her fears when it came her turn to approach the godar.

They passed a group of men gathered around two younger men who were playing chess, a game similar to their traditional pastime of hnefatafl. Loud wagers were being made on who would win, while the two opponents ignored those around them to concentrate on the carved ivory pieces.

After making a move, one young man looked up in ill-concealed triumph. He grinned around at the throng of men, his glance finally coming to rest on Disa and Agnes standing a short distance away.

His eyes grew wide, his mouth hanging open. He stared, transfixed by Agnes's beauty. It took a thump on the back to bring him back to himself.

"Wake up, Olaf! What ails you, Man?"

The other men were jeering him good-naturedly until they, too, followed his look. The entire group suddenly went silent.

Since many used the Althing as a time for courtship and spouse searching, it didn't surprise Disa when Olaf slowly rose to his feet. The look in his eyes warned her.

His opponent, though as obviously impressed by Agnes's beauty, was nonetheless more interested in finishing the game. He placed a restraining hand on Olaf's arm.

"Finish the game, Olaf, or else forfeit and give me my earnings."

Olaf reluctantly dragged his gaze away from Agnes to look at the young man sitting across from him. Honor would demand that he finish his task in order to prove himself. He slowly seated himself, his eyes following as Agnes and Disa hurried away. The last thing they heard were loud jeers when Olaf made a foolish move. The young man's concentration had obviously been broken.

They passed a booth where a man was selling bone-tipped arrows. Most of the men could make their own, but many hadn't the skill or the time. The seller was doing a thriving business.

Another booth was selling ale. Disa hurried by, anxious to gain some distance from the men who were quaffing the drink so freely. The memory of a long winter would make them eager for sport, another reason her mother had chosen not to attend the Althing before.

When the lawspeaker stood to recite the law, Disa knew it would soon be time to bring her case before the group of godar. The lawspeaker droned on for some time, reciting from memory one-third of the law. Next year he would recite another third, and the following year the final third. Although it was customary to choose another lawspeaker, few desired the job. They were already stretched to the limit by all the work required just to insure survival.

Disa and Agnes seated themselves close to the ruling group to await their turn. Many of those who went forward were angry, their voices raised loudly in protest against each other. As each case was settled, the crowd diminished until only a few remained. One of those was Horik, and he was once again watching Disa with unnerving interest.

Even though the godar would make judgments, there was

no way to enforce their decisions. The only thing that kept most people from disputing with the lawgivers was the fear of word fame. Having their names added disparagingly to the sagas would be a dreadful breach of honor. This threat was the one thing that would cause a man to fight to the death or back down from a fight. Honor, such as it was, meant everything among Disa's people.

When it came Disa's turn to speak, she rose and went forward with butterflies still dancing around in her stomach. She could feel her trembling start again and hoped that it wouldn't affect her speech. It was important to sound firm before these intimidating men.

"I wish to let it be known that this woman," she pointed to Agnes, who was trying to make herself as inconspicuous as possible, "is now a free woman."

Instant rumblings sounded among the crowd. With so much work to do on the farms, it was unusual to give thralls their freedom. Every hand was needed to work the farms, especially if one was a woman with no man to turn to.

Many stared at Disa as though she had lost all reason. The thralls attending to their duties stared with open envy.

Erik watched her unblinkingly before turning to discuss it with the other judges. They nodded their heads, turning their full perusal upon Agnes's shrinking form. She colored hotly under this heavy regard. Erik nodded. "So be it."

Disa's legs almost buckled under the weight of relief that flooded her. Although the godar couldn't have refused her decision to free her own thrall, having completed her business with the council removed a heavy load of dread. She glanced quickly around. "That is all that I have to say."

Disa retreated to her seat, and Horik took her place before the lawgivers. Disa's stomach clenched into knots. She knew what he was going to say.

Horik pointed to her. "This woman and her thrall cannot manage the farm that Leif left in their care. They have no man. I wish to take it over and keep it well until Leif's return. It would not do for the son of Erik to find his land had been left fallow and his property not cared for."

Erik glanced at Disa. "What have you to say to this?"

Disa rose to her feet, facing them with blazing eyes. Although she knew what Horik was up to, the audacity of the man fueled her fiery temper. "I am perfectly capable of caring for the land that Leif left to my father. It has been two years since my father's death, yet the farm is thriving. My father taught me well the art of caring for animals."

She refused to consider the fact that if it were not for Thorvald, she would most likely starve in the coming winter and so would her animals. There was absolutely no way that she could harvest the hay in the quantities necessary for her animals' survival.

Erik frowned, clearly in a quandary over the issue. It was his own son's property that was in dispute, and he would certainly want it kept in the best condition possible until his son's return from across the sea.

"I would remind you," Disa told them, her voice no longer quavering, "that Leif gave the land to my father and his children for two generations."

It was not unusual for a landowner to deed his land over for a couple of generations and then to want it back. Leif would be certain to be finished with his wandering by then and ready to settle down.

Disa's father had hoped to make his fortune in Greenland and then return to one of the Danish provinces. Since Disa had no husband, she had no idea what would happen to her in the coming years. Horik was actually right when he said that she couldn't farm the land alone. For the past several months, she had been trying to reason all of this out in her own thoughts, but no answer had come to her.

"Leif expected your father to have sons," Horik ranted, interrupting her thoughts. "Your father had no sons, nor will you be likely to."

Disa bridled under his assault, yet she felt the painful truth of his words. The other godar were eyeing her shrewdly, knowing that she had little chance of marrying someone from the vicinity. Disa was afraid they were leaning in Horik's favor because he had many sons to provide for. Before she could speak, Horik went on bitingly. "No man will have you, a cursed woman. At least no man in his right mind."

"Are you saying, Horik, that I am out of my mind?"

Thorvald stepped to the center of the group. His cold gaze was fixed unwaveringly on Horik. "I told you once before that the woman was mine. Perhaps you did not believe me."

Horik lost some of his bluster under the other man's stare.

"So you said, Thorvald, but I have not heard of a marriage taking place."

Without looking at Disa, Thorvald told him, "That is what I am here to rectify." His look swept past a glowering Disa and settled on the godar. "The Althing is a time for marriage contracts. I have come to announce mine to Disa Halgerdsdottir."

He looked at Disa. She scowled back at him, knowing she could not speak out against him. There was really no other way. She felt Agnes's hand slip into hers and, glancing down, noticed the sad look on her face.

Erik stood. "Then the case is settled. You really have no right to Disa's land, Horik." He smiled at Thorvald. "Since neither of you have a father here to make the arrangements, I will stand in their stead." It was more than a suggestion. He motioned Disa forward, and she reluctantly stepped to Thorvald's side.

Erik turned to Thorvald. "What is your bride price?"

Disa's eyes widened. She had forgotten the law that said it was necessary for a groom to give a bride price. Without it, the marriage contract was not legal. She peeped at Thorvald from the corner of her eyes. Whatever he gave, she would be required to give something of equal worth, and she had very little left of value. Had Thorvald remembered the bride price?

Thorvald reached into a pouch attached to his belt and pulled out a gold coin. Disa drew in a shocked breath when he turned and held it out to her. She had absolutely nothing of comparable worth.

Erik turned to Disa. "And you?"

Thinking quickly, Disa pulled the silver cross from beneath her dress. The metal was warm from resting against her skin. She clutched it tightly, her eyes meeting Thorvald's for the first time. What she saw was hardly reassuring. His blue eyes were coldly blank.

She opened her palm and handed the cross to him. He took the cross, replacing it in her hand with the gold coin.

Erik coughed slightly. "The prices are hardly equal."

Thorvald looked at him and smiled. "You forget. Disa will be giving me her land and farm as well. The prices, I think, are more than fair."

Disa opened her mouth to protest but stopped when Erik threw back his head and laughed heartily. He slapped Thorvald on the back.

"You are right when you say so." His look came to rest on Disa, and she saw the hesitation in his eyes. "I offer you Brattahlid for the marriage ceremony. Since most of Eriksfjord are here for the Althing, the wedding may as well take place soon."

Disa looked at Thorvald once again and knew that there would be no way out for her.

six

Thorvald grinned at Disa, who was pacing up and down in the confines of the great room of her home. She had really worked herself into a fine rage. He wondered if she realized how lovely she was when her eyes sparkled like the volcanoes of Iceland and her skin warmed to a golden glow just like those same volcanoes.

Periodically, she would glare at him as though she might attack him physically as well as verbally. His grin broadened, his blood warming at the mental picture it invoked.

"I cannot believe you would do such a thing without my consent," she railed for the sixth time.

Thorvald folded his arms over his chest, lifting a sardonic brow. "What would you have had me do? I gave my word to your mother, and I intend to keep it."

He wondered at the look of pain that flashed through her eyes but attributed it to the reminder of her beloved mother. He cursed himself for being so careless.

"Disa, I know Erik. He would have ruled in Horik's favor."

She whirled to face him, her hands firmly planted on her hips. "You heard him say that Horik had no right to the land."

Thorvald nodded. "That is true, but that was after he knew that I would be here to care for the land."

"You do not know that," she told him, sounding less than sure of herself.

Growing angry, Thorvald crossed the room until he could look her in the face. She took a hasty step in retreat, but he followed. "What is done, is done. I will hear no more of it."

She drew herself up to her full height and faced him toe-to-toe. "Oh, yes, you will. I have not had my say."

Gritting his teeth together, he almost snarled at her. "What do you think you have been doing for the past hour? There is no more to be said. As I told you before, what is done, is done."

He knew the exact moment she realized that she was, indeed, trapped. The fire left her eyes, and her shoulders slumped forward. He wanted to reassure her, but he wasn't exactly sure how.

"Disa," he said, placing his hands on her shoulders. "We will make this succeed. Have you not seen how well we work together? What would you do if I did not help you with the farm?"

She sighed, lifting tired eyes to his face.

He found himself with an unexpected ally when Agnes's voice joined his in support. "You know that he is right, Disa."

Disa turned to Agnes in surprise and searched her face intently for something Thorvald couldn't understand. After a time, she shook herself free from Thorvald's hold. Walking very slowly across the room, she deliberately took the gold coin she had thrown on the table earlier and placed it inside her keepsake chest. She carefully closed the lid, leaning on it for support.

When she spoke, her voice was hoarse with emotion. "We must talk, Thorvald. Alone."

Agnes's look went from one to the other. She quickly rose from her seat near the fire. "I will go for a walk."

Disa shook her head. "No, there are still too many people at the gathering, and it is not so far away. You will be safer inside. Thorvald and I will go for a walk."

Disa crossed out into the twilight first. As Thorvald joined her, she turned back toward the house. "Lock the door," she commanded, and Agnes hurried to comply, giving Disa a reassuring smile before shutting the door behind them.

Thorvald walked at Disa's side, watching her warily. Just what did she want to talk with him about? She had done enough railing at him about his deed. Surely, as he had told her, there was nothing more to say.

They walked some way before Disa finally seated herself on a small boulder. She watched a butterfly flutter by, staring after it until it was long gone. Thorvald waited patiently, knowing that she was trying to gather her thoughts.

She opened her mouth to speak, then, frowning, closed it again. He scowled. What was it that she was having such a hard time saying? They were both trapped, and they both knew it. For his part, he welcomed the chance to finally get the issue out into the open between them.

When she looked at him again, he saw the stark fear in her eyes. Believing he knew what she was thinking, his body grew rigid with anger.

"Just so that you know, I have never murdered anyone in my life. I never went a viking, and I never was involved in a blood feud."

She looked at him in surprise. Her forehead creased, and she tilted her head slightly. "I did not think that you had," she replied, making it sound more a question.

He blew out a breath and stood. Turning away from her probing look, he ground out, "I saw the fear in your eyes just now."

"I would be lying if I said that I was not afraid, but it is not for the reasons that you suggest."

Puzzled, he turned back and allowed his gaze to wander over her, coming back to rest on her eyes. "Then what do you fear? Horik will not bother you. I will see to that."

She shook her head, and he realized that the half-smile on

her face was a sad one. Growing frustrated, he seated himself beside her. He wanted to pull her around to face him more fully, but her expression was hardly encouraging.

She ducked her head, and her hair dipped forward, hiding her face from his view.

"Thorvald, I have never been with a man."

It took him a few moments to adjust his mind to her statement. Comprehension dawned. This time, he did pull her round to face him.

"If that is what is concerning you, Disa, then you need not worry. I promise I will be gentle with you."

She shook her head, refusing to meet his look. "No, you do not understand."

Growing more confused by the minute, he tipped her chin with one finger. "Then help me to understand."

"I. . ." Biting her lip, she pulled from his grasp and stood. She kept her back to him as she told him, "I do not want to be with you in that way."

He blinked rapidly, digesting what she had just said. The anger that had begun earlier now exploded. He wasn't certain exactly how he felt about Disa, but he would be hanged before he would commit himself to a celibate marriage. He got to his feet, jerking her around to meet his angry glare.

"This I refuse to do," he told her unequivocally.

She placed her hands against his chest, and he felt his heart thundering beneath her palms. He wasn't certain if it was because of his anger or the sudden knowledge that he found the woman more attractive than he had at first realized.

"Please, Thorvald," she begged softly. "At least for a time. I–I cannot give myself to you freely unless. . .unless I love you. I just cannot."

"And if you never love me?" he inquired sarcastically.

Disa looked up at him and wondered what he would say if

she told him she thought she was halfway there already. Agnes was right. He was a good man, so unlike the other men she came in contact with that she couldn't help but be attracted to him. His devastating good looks were an added bonus.

"Please, just give me time," she whispered, the words drifting off into the night air.

He let her go, taking several paces away from her. His back was as rigid as the mountains that surrounded them. Eventually, he turned to her, his look dark and forbidding.

"The winters are long, Disa," he told her, both eyes and voice devoid of emotion. "I will give you until then."

Disa swallowed hard. The thought of being closed inside a house for months on end with this decidedly male being was an alarming thought. Still, what choice did she have? She nodded her head in agreement, and Thorvald turned and stalked off for his own home.

❧

Disa sat less than relaxed in the bath at Erik's farm as Agnes poured a pitcher of water over her head. The steam from the sauna swirled around her in a white fog, reminding her of that day not so long ago when Thorvald had come to rescue her.

When Thjohilde motioned her to get out, Disa was loath to do so. Although the hot bath was meant to be relaxing on this, her wedding day, it hadn't worked. She was as tense as the string on a bow.

Agnes helped her into the rinse water. As she stepped in, the herbs floating on the top parted around her. The fragrance drifting upward from the warm water was soothing to her taut nerves. She spent as much time there as possible, but she knew she must face her destiny sometime. She climbed slowly from the tub and waited patiently as Agnes dried her.

Thjohilde lifted a dress from the bench beside the door. The white linen dress was being lent to Disa for the occasion.

Although Disa appreciated the offer, the thought of what the dress represented had made her averse to accepting the gift. Only her wish to avoid hurting Thjohilde's feelings had made her relent.

Disa allowed Thjohilde to help her on with her kirtle, adjusting the undergarment until it slid over her body and fell into soft folds around her. Agnes was ready with the overdress. The white linen draped becomingly over the kirtle, reaching almost to the floor. The dress must surely have cost a small fortune, and Disa would have been delighted to wear it if not for what it represented.

Stroking her shaking hands over the delicate embroidery that covered the garment, Disa felt her heart begin to pound an endless cadence of fear. Time was flying by all too swiftly. Only two days ago it had been Odin's day, the day to begin the Althing. Now, it was Frey's day, the day sacred to the goddess Freya, the goddess of marriage. She pulled her thoughts away from such wanderings when Agnes approached her.

"You look lovely, Disa," Agnes told her softly, and there was no mistaking the sincerity of her words.

Disa studied Agnes once again without appearing to do so, wondering if the girl had some romantic notions toward the intended groom. Although Agnes seemed pleased by Disa's state of affairs, a sadness that couldn't be missed clouded her face. Disa opened her mouth to question her about it when Thjohilde interrupted her by handing Disa the two brooches that Erik had given her as a gift.

Thjohilde smiled at Disa. "Thorvald is a good man. He will make you a fine husband. Unlike some men, he does not have the wanderlust."

Disa couldn't decide if that was a good thing or not. She attached the brooches to her dress, standing patiently while Agnes combed her hair until it shone.

She could put it off no longer. The time had come. Feeling as though she were about to be sentenced, Disa followed the other two women into Erik's great hall.

Already the celebration was in full sway. Erik sat in the high seat with Thorvald, his son, on one side and Thorvald, her intended, on the other. They were laughing at some jest when her Thorvald happened to glance up and see them.

The smile left his face; his eyes widened. He lowered his drinking horn to the table, sticking the pointed end into a loaf of bread to keep it upright. Slowly, he rose to his feet.

Erik noticed the direction of Thorvald's look and turned. The older man's lips tilted into a slow smile. He motioned the women forward, but Disa found it hard to comply with her legs shaking so badly. It seemed an eternity before she finally reached his side. Thorvald took her cold hands into his as they stood before Erik.

Since there were so few trees in Greenland to constitute a grove set apart for rituals, Erik had decided to have the cere-mony on the shores of the fjord. They made their way out-side and down to the water's edge. One of Erik's thralls had already started a fire to lend warmth to the chilling evening and to brighten the evening's twilight. The driftwood snapped and crackled, shooting sparks into the air.

Thorvald, Erik's son, slew a goat to gain the gods' atten-tion, allowing its blood to fill a bowl and handing over the animal to be used for the feast later on. Disa shivered, her stomach, already clenched into tight knots, threatening to rebel even further at the sight of these rituals for gods she no longer believed in.

The guests had assembled around the two, and now Erik took a willow branch and dipped it into the blood. With a sweeping gesture down and across, he sprayed the gathered throng with the blood as a sign of the gods' blessings upon them. Only a tiny amount landed on any one person, so well had Erik performed the ritual.

Thorvald then turned to Disa and, pulling his sword from its baldric, handed it to her. When his eyes met hers, Disa felt the hypocrisy of the moment. His giving of his family's sword into her trust signified her promise to care for it until it was time to hand it over to their own son. Face warming with color, she turned away from his look.

Agnes stepped up beside her and handed Disa the sword that Disa had sent to Erik's house earlier. It was one of the few remaining items she had left to remember her father by. Thinking of the man she had loved so dearly, she fought to keep tears from her eyes. This symbol of exchanging her father's guardianship for Thorvald's was heart wrenching.

Thorvald took the sword from Disa and placed a ring on it. He then held the sword out to her, his eyes more serious than she had ever seen them.

Fingers still shaking, Disa took the ring from the blade and placed it on her finger. Struggling with Thorvald's heavy sword, she gave him a return token in the same manner. Erik had given her the ring when he found out that she had none of her own to give. The silver circle glinted in the light of the fire.

Taking the ring, Thorvald placed it on his finger. Their eyes met, and Disa shivered at the carefully blank look on Thorvald's features.

They joined hands on the hilt of Thorvald's sword and, in a voice that shook, Disa made her vows. Thorvald did the same.

For the first time since she had entered the hall, Disa saw Thorvald's lips curl into a genuine smile. She knew the reason, and she felt herself tense in expectation of his challenge.

"So," he said in an amused voice, "whom do you think will

make it back to the hall first?"

He grinned at her soft snort. As though there would be any question. She eyed his lithe form warily. She had not been particularly looking forward to the brudh-hluap, or bride running. There was no way that she could outdistance Thorvald's long-legged stride, even if she had wanted to. Besides, it was customary for the man to win so that he could be at the feasting hall first to help his bride over the doorstep.

Although Disa no longer believed in the old gods, the thought of demons hiding near the doorway left her trembling. Christ himself had spoken of demons. If she should trip, it could be a sign of sure misfortune.

"Disa?"

Shaken out of her thoughts, she looked up at Thorvald. She didn't know what provoked her, but she found herself telling him mischievously, "I will see you at the hall."

She just had time to see his mouth open in surprise before she had turned and was running for the hall. She could hear the loud cheers of the crowd from behind.

She should have known better. Hearing Thorvald's thundering footsteps close behind, Disa turned her head slightly to look back. He was so close he could have reached out and touched her. She saw his challenging grin when he overtook her, passing her so swiftly that she had no hope of catching him. When she finally stumbled toward the door, her breathing came more rapidly than normally would happen from such a small amount of exertion.

Thorvald barred the doorway with his sword, keeping her from entering. Grinning victoriously, he swept her off her feet and into his arms. Startled, Disa wrapped her arms around his neck. It was customary for the groom to help the bride over the doorstep so that she couldn't trip and thus allow the demons their mischief, but she hadn't expected this. Thorvald's laughing eyes met hers. The sound around Disa seemed to evaporate as she stared into his eyes. Ever so slowly, the laughter died out of his face.

"Thorvald!"

Erik's voice startled them both. Turning to face the other man, Thorvald allowed Disa to slide to her feet, yet he kept one arm firmly around her.

"Come along, Boy," Erik thundered. "Show us a sign of your virility!"

Disa could have cheerfully crawled into a hole. Her cheeks grew hot with embarrassment.

Thorvald released her with a laugh and reached for the sword that Erik returned to him. Thorvald took his sword and, with the others in the room cheering loudly, he buried the blade into the main upright beam holding the roof. The blade sliced like butter into the wood, leaving a deep scar. The men in the room roared their approval. Thorvald turned back to Disa. "I will take my drink now," he told her, grinning.

Having lost the race, it was required of Disa's bridal party to serve the drinks to the groom's party. Since Disa's bridal party consisted only of her and Agnes, the task seemed daunting with so many guests present.

Thjohilde came to her rescue once again by offering her own thralls' service. That being accomplished, the party waxed louder with the flowing of the mead.

Disa poured a small amount of mead into the kasa and handed the two-handled cup to Thorvald. Without this act, the marriage would not be legal. She had to swallow twice before she could speak any words in his honor. Never having attended a wedding before, she had no idea what to say. Although Thjohilde had instructed her during her bath about the marriage and wifely duties, she had neglected to mention the kasa ceremony.

"May you live long and be strong until the day you are finally laid to rest," Disa said.

Thorvald grinned and took the cup, his eyes meeting Disa's once again over the rim. She couldn't understand the message she saw there. All she knew was that it caused her an instant moment of panic.

"May Odin bless our marriage, and may Freya give us strong sons." His words caused a little niggle of fear to worm its way into her heart. What exactly was he saying? He had promised to give her time before consummating their marriage, but the look in his eyes and the toast he had proclaimed gave the lie to his words.

He took a sip from the cup, then handed it to Disa. Though it was expected of her, there was no way that she would make a toast to Freya. She glanced around at the assembled throng and took her courage into hand.

"May God bless our marriage and keep it pure," she said softly but clearly.

The quiet in the room was profound. Disa noticed Erik's frown of disapproval, but then she caught Thjohilde's smile of approbation.

"Come," Thjohilde called quickly, "it is time to eat."

The crowd came alive at her words. Disa and Thorvald were seated at a table together with Erik at its head. The appetizing aroma of grilled fish filled the air, making Disa's empty insides react.

Disa thought she couldn't be embarrassed any further, but she was wrong. Erik came to place a small hammer of Thor's in her lap. Her cheeks burned with mortification when he invoked a blessing on her fertility. Chancing a glance at Thorvald, she noticed the slow grin that came to his face.

After asking the blessing, Erik then called for more food to be brought out. Although she was hungry, Disa knew that she would never be able to eat a bite without becoming ill. Her insides were twisting and turning enough to churn butter.

A slow pounding began in her temples and proceeded around her skull and beyond. She massaged her scalp, trying to relieve some of the pressure.

"Here, let me."

Before she could stop him, Thorvald stood and gently pushed her hands away. He began massaging her head with slow, circular movements. She tensed, but it wasn't long before she felt herself responding to his gentle touch. She drifted on a tide of euphoria as his hands moved from her head to her shoulders. Before long, her body had relaxed and the pain in her head had ceased.

"Bring the lights," Erik called. "It is time to put the wedding couple to bed."

Disa's headache returned with a vengeance.

seven

Through a painful haze, Disa saw Thorvald approach Erik. How had she ever gotten herself into this? She would lay no blame on her mother, for Halgerd had never shown her anything but love and kindness. What had started out as Halgerd's expression of love had turned into Disa's foolish mistakes. She should have sent Thorvald on his way in the beginning instead of even considering his words. She should never have agreed to their partnership in the first place.

Erik glanced her way and then at Agnes, his face sober. He nodded his head at Thorvald. Erik then mingled with the crowd and soon the whispers started. When looks turned her way, Disa wondered what Thorvald had told the older man.

Thorvald returned to her side and reached out a hand to help her to her feet. She was in no state to refuse him. Besides, with all eyes watching, she didn't dare.

"Have no fear," Thorvald whispered into her ear, sending shivers down her spine. "I have convinced Erik that due to your and Agnes's status among the people, it would be best not to undress you here."

Disa closed her eyes in relief. She had been dreading this part of the ceremony that would symbolize a sexual union. So much of her people's pagan practices were a familiar part of her life, and at times, she had no idea what would please the Lord. Sometimes her soul cried out to her that an action was wrong, but at other times, she wasn't as certain. Would she ever truly know what God thought was wrong and right? If only she could have access to the Word of God as Agnes had. How she envied the younger woman. She glanced up at Thorvald, noting his sardonic smile.

Thjohilde approached their table and smiled. "Agnes will stay with me tonight," she told them.

Disa felt real panic. She and Thorvald alone. The thought brought a metallic taste of fear to her mouth.

"Thank you," Thorvald answered for her. In truth, Disa couldn't have spoken if she had tried.

Holding out her hand, Thjohilde smiled reassuringly at Disa. "Come. Agnes and I together will prepare you."

Disa locked eyes with Thorvald, swallowing hard at the look she found in his. She quickly turned away to join Thjohilde. It was good of the woman to act in her mother's place, and she was thankful; but right now, Disa wanted nothing more than to be alone. The ability to keep her confident mask in place was deteriorating by the minute.

She followed the other two women to Disa's house. Since her land was in reality Leif's, her farm was much closer to Brattahlid than most farms. In this instance, she could have wished it much farther away, though then she would probably have been required to be Erik's guest. That thought caused her to hurry her feet onward.

What exactly would Thorvald expect of her on this, their wedding night? He had given her until winter before they would consummate their marriage, but would he hold to that promise? In the next instant, she realized that Thorvald was a man of honor. He would never go back on his word. Hadn't his promise to her mother shown that to be true? She felt a sudden peace at this knowledge; and for the first time in several hours, her head ceased to throb.

Once again, Thjohilde had been kind enough to provide her with a wedding garment. The nightdress was of snow-white linen with intricate gold embroidery depicting Freyr with the giantess Gerd. This symbol of fertility brought a warm rush of color to her cheeks. Although beautiful, more beautiful than any garment she had ever seen, Disa wanted to rip it off and change it for her own plain kirtle, but again, she couldn't bring herself to hurt Thjohilde by rejecting her gift.

Agnes took the comb from the shelf and smoothed Disa's hair with long, tender strokes. Disa smiled at the girl, knowing that she was trying to relieve Disa's tension. Under Agnes's ministering touch, she finally began to relax.

"He is a good man," Agnes reminded Disa.

Disa couldn't disagree, but she hadn't yet told Agnes the truth about their situation. For some reason, she was reluctant to let Agnes know that theirs was to be an unfulfilled marriage, at least for a time.

Thjohilde pulled back the furs on Disa's sleeping bench. She arranged a statue of Freyr and Gerd among the covers. Agnes and Disa exchanged quick glances. So close had they become that without saying a word, when Thjohilde wasn't looking, Agnes quickly removed the statue and hid it in the apron of her dress. She could return it on the morrow, but in the meantime, neither of them wanted idols in their home.

Before long, they heard the ribald laughter of the witnesses coming up the hill. Disa took a deep breath, her anxious eyes meeting Agnes's briefly.

Thjohilde touched Disa's cheek with her fingers, smiling slightly. "Thankfully our people no longer hold to the tradition of witnessing the marriage act. You will have your privacy."

Disa heaved a sigh of relief. What Thjohilde said was certainly true. Disa could not have borne such an act, which would have allowed no possibility for holding off the marriage bed as she and Thorvald had agreed upon. She reluctantly got into bed.

Without knocking, the six men and women who were act-ing as witnesses entered the house. Their drunken hilarity grated on Disa's already raw nerves.

Erik stumbled over the doorstep, righting himself with a self-deprecating laugh. He threw a lecherous grin at his wife, but she ignored him.

Something Agnes said came back clearly to Disa at that instant. She had said that the Scriptures forbade a woman to refuse her mate his husbandly rights except by mutual agree-ment, then only for a short season.

The thought was an unwelcome one. She had no right to deny Thorvald his husbandly rights, but then she satisfied herself with the thought that they had made an agreement for a season. Summers were short enough here; but all of a sudden, they seemed much shorter.

Thorvald followed the others into the room. Although she could tell he was not drunk, it was obvious the mead had affected him. His gaze moving slowly over her was filled with a feverish glitter. Her heart that had felt so peaceful now sud-denly went wild like a berserker.

Still fully clothed, Thorvald joined her on the bed. With the witnesses able to testify later to their union, they had ful-filled this part of the ceremony.

Erik swept a drunken bow. "And now we will leave you two alone. Do not do anything that I would not do."

The others in the room roared with mirth, slapping him on the back. They stumbled back through the doorway, exit-ing the house on a wave of laughter. Agnes was the last to leave. Her look met Disa's, but her face was carefully empty of emotion. Disa had no idea what the other girl might be thinking or feeling. Agnes carefully closed the door after her.

At the door's thud, Disa slowly turned to face Thorvald. He was watching her guardedly, his feelings veiled behind a suddenly blank stare. They could hear the sound of the others' hilarity fading into the distance, then they were alone.

Disa had no idea what to say. She turned away from his intent look, ducking her head forward. Her hair fell over her shoulder, hiding her face from his view. She felt him move. With a finger, he pulled back her hair so that he could better see her face.

"Disa?"

What did he want her to say? She took a deep breath, turning back to face him.

"I will remember my promise," he told her, his voice a husky whisper.

It was several seconds before she could find the voice to answer him.

"Thank you," she returned, her voice no less husky.

"But right now it will be extremely hard." There was amusement lurking in his voice, but something else as well.

She glanced at him in surprise and saw that he meant it. He truly found her attractive. Feelings she had never experienced before assailed her. Feelings of an age-old power she had never heretofore possessed. The power of a woman over a man.

His blue eyes darkened until they were almost black. When he next spoke, the amusement had fled. "You are mine, Disa."

The intensely spoken words sent the butterflies flitting around in her stomach once again. With that spoken, he got up and walked out the door.

❧

Thorvald didn't know how he had managed to get out the door with his mind intact. He had been a long time without a woman, and now this particular one was his wife. The next several months were going to be pure torture if things kept on this way.

He couldn't say when he had first noticed that he had become attracted to Disa, but he knew with certainty that he was. Was it possible that he could be in love? He scoffed at the idea. If anything, his people based their marriages on political alliances and lust. Certainly not love. At least he had never seen it. Even his own mother had divorced his father but, for what reason, they would never say. It had happened more than eighteen years ago.

Divorce was rampant among his people; and though he was used to it, the thought of Disa doing so to him left him vaguely disturbed. He would not give up easily what belonged to him.

He went to the barn and settled himself in the hay. This, then, would be his bed, at least for the night. He sighed heavily, wishing it could be otherwise. Getting Disa's figure out of his mind would be an exercise in self-control. She had looked so lovely in her white linen nightdress, her hair flowing around her in a soft, shining haze. He closed his eyes tightly, trying to shut out the image, but it became even clearer.

Lying back, he stared through the darkness to the ceiling above. Pulling one leg up and folding his arms behind his head, he gave serious consideration to the coming months ahead. He had given Disa an ultimatum, but would he have the courage to force the issue if she chose to ignore it? Facing an enemy held more appeal to him than such a thought.

Perhaps there was another way. His lips curled slowly as he thought of how he might change things to his advantage. Surely if given the right incentive, Disa would yield. And that incentive was for her to fall in love with him. Was not that what she had said? She couldn't give herself to a man unless she loved him. Where she had gotten such decidedly un-Norselike thoughts he had no idea, but had them she did.

Well, if he could tame a wild horse, perhaps he could do the same with his woman. His smile broadened into a grin. He would have to wait and see, but he had no doubt of the victor.

❧

In the morning, Disa was waiting when Agnes and Thjohilde joined her. She smiled at Thjohilde and hugged her friend. "I missed you."

Disa realized that was the wrong thing to say when she noticed Thjohilde's peculiar look. Hastily trying to rectify it, she laughed. "Thorvald is not as adept at helping me with my hair."

Thjohilde's eyebrows lifted slightly, but she shrugged. "Do you have a hustrulinet, Disa? If not, I can provide you with one."

Disa produced the white linen head covering that her mother had made especially for her in the last days of her life. Halgerd had not had the time to prepare a wedding gown, nor a wedding nightdress, but she had been determined to provide the head covering.

Agnes once again took up the comb and began stroking Disa's long hair. Today it would be plaited and covered, a sign that she was a married woman. Disa would miss the way her hair had always blown freely in the wind. It had always given her a feeling of being unrestrained, free like the wild ponies back home in Norway.

Agnes wound the long braid into a topknot, attaching the hustrulinet with two long pins made from bone. She stood back to survey her handiwork and smiled at Disa. "You look different," she said quietly.

"I do not feel different," Disa returned.

Thjohilde laughed. "That will come with time. Right now you are still young and marriage is still new. Soon, you will become as one flesh." She came to an abrupt halt, her look suddenly distant. She stood thus for some time before she shook herself and smiled at Disa. "So tell me of your dreams last night."

Disa shrugged. "I had no dreams." After the exhausting day and the climax of the evening, Disa had fallen into a deep sleep and slept soundly.

She was surprised at the other woman's sudden frown. "None?"

Disa shook her head slowly, her forehead creased. "No. Why?"

Thjohilde's look was serious. "That is not a good thing. No dreams means you will have no children." Disa had forgotten that particular superstition. Was there some truth in the words of her people? After all, such thoughts had been around far longer than Disa had been alive. She tried to impart some of her growing faith in the Lord. "If the Lord so wills, then that is what will be. But I do not believe that to be so."

Thjohilde chewed on her bottom lip pensively. She shook her head, mumbling to herself. "This is not a good thing."

Disa well understood the older woman's dilemma and once again gave thanks that she had Agnes to give her the Word of God. Perhaps in time she would share them with Thjohilde as well.

"Come, Child," Thjohilde said, snapping her fingers. "Let us finish getting you ready. We saw Thorvald on our way up, and I sent him on to Brattahlid. He will be waiting to give you your morning gift."

The morning gift had totally slipped Disa's mind. She wondered if Thorvald would remember or even know about it.

It seemed he had. When they entered the hall at Brattahlid, Thorvald approached Disa and handed her a beautiful set of brooches. She was awed by their worth and beauty. These were made not of silver but of gold and were intricately carved with flowing dragons. She wondered where he had gotten such ornaments.

She took them from him, smiling hesitantly. His expression was earnest, his look warm. "For you, Disa. My beautiful wife."

Her mouth parted at his words. Did he truly see her in such a way? Was it possible? Or did he wish something from her? She frowned with sudden suspicion.

Taking his keys from his ring, Thorvald handed them to her. The keys to his chests and storerooms at his farm. Although required by law, she hadn't expected this. Since she wouldn't be living at his farm, she wanted to give them back; but she didn't because Erik suddenly joined them. He smiled broadly at them.

"So, now your marriage is legal. Come, break the fast with us."

Although both the Althing and weddings normally took a week, the summers in Greenland were far too short to waste on frivolities. Still, many folks would take advantage of the situation and stay to revel with the others, much to their detriment later on. Disa had seen the results of last year's poor planning by some. It would seem they had no wish to remember any lessons from the long winter they had just survived.

As for herself and Thorvald, they would be leaving soon after breaking the fast. There was still much to do, although many here would assume that they were leaving so quickly for another reason.

Disa blushed, and Thorvald lifted an enquiring brow at her. She ignored him, instead joining Erik and Thjohilde at their table.

She had to step carefully over prone bodies still sleeping

off the effects of the previous night's merrymaking. It amazed Disa that Erik was on his feet so early after imbibing so much. Famished after going so long without food, Disa enjoyed the flaky fish placed before her. She wrinkled her nose with distaste when Thorvald chose seal meat. She had never liked the taste of seal, much preferring whale meat, although it was harder to come by.

More guests arrived as the morning progressed, while those sleeping in the great hall began to rouse. They were not guests of her wedding, but guests of Erik, who opened his house freely to anyone who visited the area. Before long it was plain to see that they were on their way to another round of festivity. Thorvald joined a group of men playing a game of hnefatafl. Studying his broad form as he fingered one of the carved playing pieces, Disa was surprised by the fierce pride that swamped her when she thought of his now belonging to her.

At one point the flytings began. Disa supposed it was inevitable, but she had never liked the insult contests. Still, it was a favorite part of any merrymaking. Far worse, she supposed, were the lying stories.

She felt a presence beside her and looked up. Horik stood glaring down at her.

"So," he grated, "Thorvald figured out a way to get your land for himself, hmm?" He reached out a hand and stroked her cheek. "My son was not good enough for you, huh?"

She slapped his hand away, and his look became more threatening. He leaned down until their faces were too close for Disa's liking. Already his breath reeked of ale. Horik was suddenly jerked around to face Thorvald's wrathful figure

"Get away from my wife," Thorvald hissed.

Erik rose at the same time, and Horik realized his mistake. It was unseemly to cause strife as the guest of another man.

Nodding to Erik, he threw one dark look Thorvald's way before walking away. Thorvald seated himself at Disa's side.

Shaking from her own anger, Disa avoided looking at him. His narrowed look fixed on her, but she chose to ignore his unasked question. She was certain, though, that it would come sooner or later. She couldn't lie to him, but she dreaded explaining what Horik had said. She had seen Thorvald's temper, and she didn't relish the idea of being its cause.

In one corner of the room, a wrestling match soon ensued. She watched Horik challenge the winner. Horik was a large man, but the two opponents seemed equally matched.

She turned to say something to Thorvald and found him intently watching the contest. She turned back in time to see Horik best the other man. Horik placed his hands on his hips and challenged all comers. Though many jeered, none were quick to take up the dare. None, that was, save Thorvald.

He rose slowly to his feet, his eyes meeting Horik's across the room. The other man's eyes glittered with feeling, but Thorvald's face was set with calm self-confidence.

"Come, Thorvald!" Horik yelled. "If you dare."

Disa reached out a hand to stop him, but he shook off her touch. He crossed to where Horik stood. Folding his arms across his chest, Thorvald asked, "What rules, Horik?"

Horik grinned crookedly, his eyes gleaming with menace. "None, Thorvald."

The room suddenly went still, all revelry ceasing as the guests realized that the two men were about to pit themselves in a serious brawl. Murmurs started as people began to wager on the outcome. Though Thorvald exceeded Horik in height by several inches, Horik had the advantage of added girth.

Horik lunged at Thorvald. The breath rushed out of Thorvald as Horik's body met his. Horik's beefy arms wrapped around Thorvald's lean waist, and he struggled to bring Thorvald to the ground. Thorvald planted his feet more firmly and soon had Horik in a headlock.

They continued to grapple, both men sweating and grunting. It soon became evident that Horik, seasoned brawler though he was, was no match for his opponent.

Suddenly, Thorvald kicked Horik's feet out from under him. The man went crashing to the floor. Thorvald was on him in an instant. Using his forearm, Thorvald pinned Horik by the neck to the floor. Horik's face grew redder as Thorvald continued to press his hold.

Disa came to her feet intent on intervening, but Erik held her back. Even coming from across the room, Thorvald's voice rang with clarity. "Touch my wife again, and I will kill you."

eight

The weeks passed, and Disa grew accustomed to her husband's presence around the farm. Although he continued to live in his isolated cottage, he made the long trek every morning to attend to Disa's farm and animals.

She and Agnes had taken to going to Thorvald's home at least once each week to care for his needs as well. They discovered very little to do because Thorvald indeed could look out for himself.

Before returning to his farm each evening, Thorvald ate the supper meal with the two women. At first, he would leave as soon as Agnes began her customary recitation of Scripture for Disa each evening; but as the days slipped by, he began to linger. The words seemed to fascinate him as much as they did Disa. Unless, she mused, there was another attraction. Was Thorvald hanging on to the Word of God or merely spellbound by Agnes's beauty?

Disa found herself looking forward to evenings with Thorvald more than she probably should have. Trying not to make it obvious, she often watched him as he sat doing some chore or listening to Agnes's stories from the Scriptures. Disa found it increasingly difficult to banish her husband from her thoughts.

"Disa, have you seen my knife?"

She looked up from her work at the kitchen table, startled by his sudden appearance. "Knife?"

"My knife with the bone handle. The one I use to process the fish. It is not where I left it."

Disa frowned. "I have not seen it." She turned to Agnes, taking the bucket of goat's milk from her hands. "Have you?"

Agnes shook her head. "I have not seen it lately. The last time that I saw it was where you left it behind the barns."

Brows puckering, Thorvald placed his fists on his hips. "I know that I left it there." He shook his head slightly, turning back to the door. "If you find it, let me know. It is my favorite."

Shrugging, Disa turned back to the task of making the cheese. She hefted the large iron pot onto the chain hanging from the ceiling. Having made certain that the fire had reached the right heat, she slowly poured the goat's milk into the cauldron. She noticed the scar on the side of the iron pot and smiled. Thorvald had fixed the cauldron to where it was almost as good as new. Was there anything her husband could not do?

She remembered the morning after her wedding, and the smile fled from her face. For a moment, she had been certain that Thorvald was going to kill Horik on the spot. Not a man would have challenged him, for it was illegal to touch another man's wife in the way that Horik had touched her. She shivered, remembering Horik's lecherous eyes. She had thought that Thorvald was about to choke the man to death when he suddenly released him and got to his feet. While Horik coughed and choked on the ground, Thorvald had calmly walked away. It was one more facet of Thorvald's personality that Disa had not witnessed before. His possessiveness frightened her.

"It is time for the vell." Agnes's voice brought Disa back from her morbid reflections. Crossing the kitchen, Disa removed the vell from the brine solution and added the curdling agent to the simmering milk.

Agnes eyed her curiously. "You seem to have much on your mind."

"There is still so much to do," Disa hedged, refusing to share her thoughts.

Pulling up a stool, Agnes continued to stir the curdling milk. "Soon," she said, "the long darkness will come. And the cold."

"That is true."

Disa had been thinking of little else. Winter was quickly approaching, and she was still no nearer to deciding whether she could love her husband. Thorvald watched her with a "biding my time" look that made her clumsy when she was around the man.

"What will Thorvald do then?"

Disa blinked at Agnes uncomprehendingly. "Do?"

"About going back and forth between the farms. That would surely be dangerous."

Disa hadn't really given the matter much thought. She had been content with matters the way they stood, supposing that they would continue indefinitely. But then, perhaps that was what Thorvald had been trying to tell her by putting a winter limitation on his patience.

She used a ladle to remove the curds to the draining cloth. What Agnes said made sense. There was no way that Thorvald could continue caring for two farms with the winter cold upon the land. It would be too much to ask of him. Sighing, she decided that she was going to have to discuss with Thorvald what was to be done this coming winter.

After placing the drained curds into the wooden cheese molds, Disa wiped her hands on a towel. She left Agnes placing the weight rocks on the molds and went in search of Thorvald. She found him behind the barns bent over his work. He scarcely glanced up, continuing to fillet the fish that he had caught earlier.

Disa hesitated, not certain how to broach the subject.

Noting her hesitation, he threw the knife into the fillet board, making its point stick into the wood, and wiped his hands on a rag. Dropping the rag on the board as well, he lifted an inquiring eyebrow in her direction. "You wanted something?"

Now that she was here, she was reluctant to bring up the subject. Frankly, she was afraid of what he might decide. "You have found your knife then?" she asked, delaying her real reason for approaching him.

"No, this is another." Amusement lurked in his eyes, and she had the strangest feeling that he knew exactly what was on her mind.

"Perhaps I left my knife at the wedding feast," he suggested.

The reminder sent color to her cheeks, and she paused before responding. Thorvald waited for her to continue.

"I was wondering what your plans are for the winter," she finally managed to say.

He crossed his arms over his chest, his sardonic look making her grit her teeth.

"Plans?" he asked softly. "What plans can I have? There is very little that can be done here in the winter. I believe that is what I tried to tell you. The nights are very long, and there is no way that I will be staying in the barn with the sheep, as warm as it may be."

Disa wrapped her arms around her waist, suddenly uncertain. "But you have your own farm to care for."

Lifting one foot to the rock beside him and laying a forearm against his bent leg, he shook his head. "Your farm is by far the larger. I haven't many animals to care for. I have already added them to yours."

She looked at him in surprise. "But. . ."

"There are no buts, Disa. I will leave my farm for the winter and reside here. I thought I had made myself plain on the matter."

Disa's anger began to rise. Of all the arrogant, demanding. . .

She ran out of words to complete the thought. "And what of your own farm? What will happen to it?"

"It will still be there when spring comes. I have very few animals because I have made most of my living by hunting and fishing. That has made it easy to forsake my farm for such long periods."

She should have realized. He didn't look like a farmer in the first place. What would it be like to be shut up with this man for months on end? And what of Agnes?

"Agnes will be living with us," she told him plainly. If she had hoped that might deter him, she was to be disappointed. His slow smile shook her composure more than a little bit, making her wonder again if he found the other woman attractive. But then, what man wouldn't?

"I have no problem with that. I had assumed that to be the case."

So he had already figured this out, had he? Her eyes narrowed. The alien feelings twisting her insides were strangely akin to jealousy, a sin she had never thought to experience.

Thorvald stepped toward her and placed his hands on her shoulders. Her thoughts scattered like chaff in the wind. She looked a long way up into his face and saw something in his eyes that left her with an oddly warm feeling beneath her breastbone.

"Disa," he entreated softly, "you have had several weeks to decide. I had hoped that you had gotten used to my presence and that we could be friends."

Her eyelashes flickered, then dropped to cover her eyes. The truth was, she did consider him a friend. He had done so much for her and Agnes already, all without complaining or arguing. Although their arrangement had been a bargain to begin with, Disa believed that Thorvald would give his life for her if necessary.

When she glanced back up at him, he accurately read the softening of her features. He pulled her forward until her lips were inches from his. "You do not need to fear me, Disa. I would never hurt you. You know that, do you not?"

His whispered words weakened her legs until she had to lean against him for support. His eyes darkened until she could see her own reflection in their dark depths. He started to dip his head forward, causing Disa's heart to pound heavily. Realizing that she hadn't answered him, he pulled back with obvious reluctance. He searched her face, trying to read her thoughts.

She felt certain that she could trust him, yet what did she really know about him? They had been married for several weeks now, but she knew no more about him than she had on the night they were married. He kept his thoughts and feelings well hidden most of the time. Would he tell her about his past if she asked?

"Thorvald, tell me about yourself." At his frown, she hurried on. "Where is your family? Where are you from?"

He released her, pushing slightly away. He turned away, refusing to look her in the eye. "What you really want to know is whether I truly murdered someone, is it not?"

She could hear the pain in his voice. Laying a hand on his arm, she denied his charge. "I only want to know something about the man I married."

He glanced at her hand resting on his arm, then back to her face. She thought he was going to refuse, but then he sighed heavily and leaned back against the rock where she had sat earlier.

"My family is from Norway. When my father heard about the land in Iceland, he moved us there." He shifted to the side, motioning for her to have a seat. "Life is hard in Iceland, even more so than here. At least here we do not have to worry about the ground shaking and the mountains spewing."

He smiled at her, a genuine smile, and she returned it, oddly content to be with him.

"My family was involved in a blood feud." His look turned outward as his memories came flooding forth. "I was in the wrong place at the wrong time," he continued. "I do not know who killed Hoffnik, but it was not I."

Disa listened to his story with mixed feelings of horror and pity. How had Thorvald managed to grow up to be such a gentle man amid a world of such violence? Surely she had seen his violent side; but for the most part, he had been nothing but kind. "Then how were you considered an outlaw?"

Thorvald glanced back at her. "Because someone saw me with the body and only that morning we had been in a brawl."

Disa studied him curiously. There had to be more to his story than that. "Over what?"

He seemed reluctant to say, and she grew more curious. "Thorvald? Over what?"

She was surprised to see color steal into his cheeks, and then it came to her with perfect clarity. "It was a woman, was it not?"

He didn't deny it, but neither did he confirm her guess.

"Anyway," he went on, "the Althing found me guilty; but since it could not be proved that I did it, I was sentenced to outlawry for only three years, at which time I may return to Iceland."

Disa didn't like the look that came to his eyes, making them once again an icy blue. "You will not go back, surely."

He faced her fully, a frown forming on his face. "At first I had thought so, but now I am not so certain."

He stood and pulled her to her feet with him, wrapping

her in his arms. Startled, Disa opened her mouth to object, but he laid a finger against her lips.

"We could have a good life together. Here. You and I."

She watched the warmth return to his eyes, a warmth that reached out and embraced her, too. When his glance focused on her lips, her heart skipped a beat, then thrummed painfully against her ribs. He moved his head forward slowly, but once again stopped. Releasing her, he pulled his knife from the board and began slicing the fish to dry. She wondered what had caused him to stop, knowing with a woman's intuition that he had been about to kiss her. Her lips still tingled with the thought, her legs shaking like blood jelly.

"Disa," Agnes called as she approached them. "We are nearly out of wood for the fire. Should I start using the peat?"

Her friend's unexpected appearance told Disa why Thorvald hadn't kissed her. He glanced quickly at Disa before answering Agnes himself. "No, I will bring you some more wood. I have a stack of driftwood out behind the house."

He paused beside Disa, giving her a look that could have melted ice in the fjords. Then he threw a cursory glance Agnes's way and left.

Frowning, Disa watched him disappear around the side of the house. It bothered her that his mere touch could reduce her thoughts to mush.

Agnes cleared her throat. "I am sorry, Disa. I did not mean to interrupt."

Her wits rattled, it took Disa a moment to gather her thoughts. She smiled reassuringly. "It is no matter. Are we ready for the next batch of milk?"

Agnes nodded, and on shaky legs, Disa turned to walk back to the house with her. They reached the inside only to find Thorvald already there. He dropped a stack of wood beside the fire and turned to leave, accidentally stepping into Agnes as he did so. He reacted quickly, reaching out to steady her.

When they exchanged smiles, Disa felt again that twisting pain of jealousy. Her suspicions began to rise. Was it an accident, or had Agnes planned it? And had she deliberately interrupted them earlier to keep Thorvald from kissing her?

Ashamed of such thoughts, Disa turned away; but the thought lingered that Agnes was a beautiful woman. And Thorvald had shown that he was not immune to the Englishwoman's beauty.

For the rest of the day, Disa felt put out about the whole situation. She vacillated between the belief that Thorvald cared for her in some small way and the belief that perhaps his caring was merely that of a man's desire for a woman. In that case, any woman would do. Even Agnes. Especially Agnes.

Tired from a long day of making cheese and discouraged into the bargain, Disa allowed Agnes to fix the evening meal while she retreated to the outside to get some fresh air. The smoke in the house was thicker than normal from all of the cooking they had done earlier. It was cloying, making Disa's stomach do somersaults.

ɬ

From his position leaning against the house, Thorvald watched Disa come outside and walk to the edge of the hill near her home. She breathed deeply of the cool night air, her silhouette relaxed and poised.

The sun would soon be dipping below the horizon more fully and for much longer periods of time. Already the first stars had appeared in the sky, and the air was growing colder. Winter was moving in quickly.

Thorvald joined her. He could see her tense against his unexpected intrusion into her solitude. Though he didn't touch her, he felt her presence keenly. Her breathing deepened at his nearness, but she refused to look at him.

"The food will soon be ready," she told him, and he didn't miss the soft quaver in her voice.

A grunt was his only answer. He wondered what she might be thinking. For so long, she had believed herself uncomely, especially to men. Now with his sudden attention, she seemed restless, as though she were waiting for something to happen.

He stood behind her, his breath fanning across her neck, making her shiver. He picked up her long braid from her back, twisting it gently in his fingers.

"Was she beautiful?"

He was caught off guard for a moment by the question until he remembered their earlier conversation. He hadn't wanted to tell her about the other woman, but he knew that he couldn't hide the facts forever. Better that she heard the story from him. Erik and many of the others had already heard a version of the tale from some visitors from Iceland. He was surprised that Disa hadn't, but then she had stayed hidden away so much of the time.

"I don't remember," he answered quietly. He heard her soft snort and grinned to himself. If he didn't know better, he would think her jealous.

"I do not believe that," she told him flatly.

He slowly turned her to face him. When she looked up at him, he could read the skepticism on her face.

"It was a long time ago."

She placed her palms against his chest, and he felt again the increased tempo of his heartbeat. He wanted more than anything right now to finish what they had started that afternoon.

"Not so long ago," she argued.

He had no idea what to say to her. "Woman," he said with

some exasperation, "you talk too much."

With that, he closed his lips over hers. When she tried to pull away, he wrapped her more fully in his embrace. He felt her resistance begin to crumble, and then she was suddenly returning his kiss in a way that left him shaken.

The door opened, and she broke from his embrace. He reached to pull her back despite Agnes's presence, but Disa quickly sidestepped him.

"Supper is ready," Agnes told them, her curious gaze resting first on Disa, then on Thorvald. Disa quickly entered the house. Taking a deep, calming breath, Thorvald followed.

The meal was quiet. Disa merely picked at her food, never raising her eyes above her plate. Thorvald was uncertain how to treat the situation. Nothing had really changed between them; yet since their encounter, Disa had been studiously avoiding him. He was fairly certain that Disa was at least attracted to him, but love was another matter. And she had been specific about that being a requirement before she would be willing to be his wife in every sense of the word.

Disa's wolf pup growled from his spot near the fire. Though a scrawny little thing, the beast had heart. He had survived an ordeal that few men would have lived through. Thorvald had given him up for dead long ago, but the animal had proven him wrong.

A thunderous knocking sounded on the door. The three in the room exchanged glances. Thorvald rose swiftly to his feet to answer the summons.

Erik's son, Thorvald, stood outside. He glanced at Thorvald, then at Disa.

"I need to speak to you outside."

Thorvald heard Disa's sharp intake of breath. Nodding his head, he followed Erik's son out the door, firmly closing it behind him. He hadn't liked the look on the other man's face. Something was seriously wrong. "What is it, Thorvald?"

Thorvald Eriksson pulled a knife from his belt. He handed it over. "My father sent me. Is this knife yours?"

Surprised, Thorvald turned the instrument over in his hands. He looked up. "It is. Where did you get it?"

The man's face was grim. "It was taken out of Horik's body."

nine

Disa warily eyed Thorvald's pacing figure. He was like a caged wolf and just about as approachable. As she helped Agnes to clear the table of their suddenly terminated meal, she noticed that Agnes was watching him just as guardedly.

"It makes no sense," Disa told him angrily. "They cannot believe that you killed Horik."

He flicked her a brief glance and continued pacing. "Can they not? Was it not I who threatened the man's life?"

Disa handed Agnes the platter with the remains of the meat. Picking up the drinking cups, she answered, "Had you wanted to kill him, you could have done so the morning of our wedding and no one would have questioned your right to do so." She handed Agnes the cups and sat down close to the table.

Thorvald stopped his pacing to lean both hands against the wood-paneled wall. He lifted his eyes to the ceiling, his jaw clenching and unclenching.

"Erik has called for a stefna. When the judges get here, they will decide whether I am guilty."

"But you are not." There was no doubt whatsoever in Disa's mind.

Thorvald turned to look at her. She could see by the relaxing of his posture that her words had done much to soothe his inflamed temper. He gave her a half-smile.

"I thank you for your belief in me. And for your concern." He picked up his cloak and sword and headed for the door.

Disa rose quickly from her seat. She couldn't bear the thought of him being alone this night. "Where are you going?"

Reaching for the door, his brows creased into a perplexed frown. "Home."

Disa bit her bottom lip before suggesting, "You could stay here." Where the words had come from she had no idea, but they could not be unsaid. Agnes's startled eyes flew to her face. Ignoring the other girl, Disa allowed herself to look Thorvald in the face.

Thorvald studied her. Disa had no idea what he could read in her look, but her own confused feelings must have been mirrored there. She watched his eyes warm with feeling before he slowly shook his head. "No," he said softly. "Not like this."

She wondered just exactly what he had meant by that, but she didn't ask. She tried to stop him one more time. Hurrying across the room, she clutched his sleeve before he could open the door. "If Horik's family has vengeance on their minds, they will try to kill you."

The warmth in his eyes intensified, and his smile was not friendly. "Let them come."

He pulled open the door and ducked into the night. Agnes came and stood beside Disa, and the two women watched his tall form disappear up the hill. Disa stood there, chewing on her lip long after he had gone. She had offered to allow him to stay, but he had refused her. Feelings of insecurity attacked her.

"He will be all right, Disa. Come, we must pray." Agnes's quiet voice drew Disa's attention.

Pray? Disa suddenly doubted whether her petitions would be effective. Why had the Lord let this happen to Thorvald, anyway? Horik was a horrible man who had deserved to die. He was known to beat his wife and female thralls. Everyone knew that, given the opportunity, Horik would have had no compunctions about killing Thorvald. Still, she felt pity for his wife. Fortunately, the woman had several sons to help care for her.

⁂

Any pity Disa had felt for Horik's wife disappeared when the woman stood before the judges in Erik's great hall and told them that she had seen Thorvald murder her husband. That she was lying was obvious to Disa, but apparently, not to the judges. Through the smoke-thickened atmosphere, she noticed them exchange brief glances.

"What have you to say, Thorvald?" Erik asked. Erik was the only one who seemed to have some doubt about the woman's words.

"The woman lies."

The gathered men conversed among themselves for several minutes. Had this been an Althing, there would have been a crowd; but having been a summoned stefna, the only people present were the judges, some of their families, Horik's family, and Thorvald and Disa.

"It is your word against the woman's," Erik told Thorvald. "Witnesses saw you with the body, and it was your knife that killed Horik."

"The witnesses lie also. I have not been to Horik's farm."

Horik's wife, Greta, smiled triumphantly at Thorvald. Disa gritted her teeth. She had a wild desire to run over to the other woman and strike the smirk from her toothless face.

Greta planted her feet apart, her hands on her hips. Although old, there was nothing infirm about her. In other circumstances, Disa might have considered her quite regal. As it was, all Disa could see was the anger that twisted the other woman's face.

"You have heard the witnesses," Greta told Erik. "Now, what is your judgment?"

Erik glanced regretfully at Thorvald. He really had no option in the face of so much testimony. That the witnesses all happened to be from Horik's family made little difference. Before Erik could speak, Thorvald stepped forward.

"I request holmgang."

Disa drew in a shocked breath. A duel. Most of the others present were equally surprised at the turn of events. It had been some time since holmgang had been enacted. Disa's heart hammered with sudden dread. When Thorvald turned to Greta, she withered under his glare.

"And you, Woman, will you do the same?"

Greta's face paled. She shook her head and turned to Erik. "It is not my word that needs to be proven," she told him, her voice holding a measure of desperation. She had no doubt expected Thorvald to be convicted and sentenced to outlawry. This unforeseen circumstance left her shaking.

Erik studied her for some time before he once again consulted with the other judges. He turned back to Greta. "Thorvald has the right to prove his innocence. You may try to best him in the holmgang yourself." There was no denying the sarcasm in his voice. "Or you may choose a man from among your witnesses."

Greta's frightened look passed over her kinsmen, finally settling on her largest son, Egill. His eyes glittered back at her, and he gave a slight nod. A slow smile settled across her mouth. "I choose Egill."

Erik sighed with resignation. "So be it." He turned to some of those standing near. "Prepare the island."

Disa's heart plummeted. There would be no onlookers allowed at the island so that a blood feud could not ensue afterward. The judges would be there to watch over the outcome and decide its fairness.

How would she ever get through the time until she knew whether Thorvald survived the duel? She wished that she could be his second, but she knew he would never allow it.

She watched him standing impassively as Erik talked with him. He nodded his head periodically at something Erik said but said little himself.

She experienced an overwhelming surge of feeling that left her suddenly breathless. Suddenly, she realized what it would mean for her if something happened to Thorvald. She needed him to help run the farm, yes, but the thought of never seeing his face again brought tears to her eyes. She truly did love the man. And what if he never knew? What if he was killed and she was not able to tell him? The thought was unbearable, but then how could she let him know?

He came to her, his eyes searching her face. "Disa?"

She had no idea what he would have said. Giving in to an impulse, she threw her arms around his neck and kissed him soundly on his lips. For a moment, he stood too surprised to move, then suddenly he wrapped her in his arms and returned her kiss with one that left Disa gasping for breath. He looked hard into her eyes before releasing her. She couldn't read his thoughts in his expressionless face.

"Thorvald! You do not need to do this," she begged him.

His dark eyes plumbed the depths of hers. He gently stroked her cheek with the back of his hand. "It is one thing to have my own honor maligned, but I will not do so with yours. Being my wife, the outcome will affect you also."

She clasped the hand resting against her cheek, her eyes burning with feeling. "What does it matter? My honor means nothing to me if it results in your death."

Surely he could tell what she was trying to say. Why couldn't she just tell him that she loved him?

"It matters to me," he argued quietly. Pulling away from her, he turned aside.

"Thorvald!"

He stopped, turning back to face her. The feelings reflected in his eyes warmed her greatly. He was not as unaffected by her own roiling emotions as she had at first supposed.

"Have a care," she whispered softly.

He nodded his head and proceeded to leave Erik's hall with the others. Disa watched him go, her heart heavy within her.

※

As they rowed out to the island, Thorvald allowed his thoughts free rein. Although he should be considering his tactics for the upcoming fight, he could only seem to focus on one thing. Disa.

A brisk wind blew across the water, causing the boat to dip and sway, but Thorvald didn't notice. What had possessed the woman to throw herself into his arms that way? What had she been thinking? The luminosity in her eyes spoke of feelings he wished he could delve into. But what exactly were those feelings?

He had no doubt that fear of the outcome of this duel played a major part in her thinking. If he should lose, in all probability he would lose his farm as part of the wergeld demanded by law. By right of marriage, Greta could demand Disa's farm in payment as well.

If he lost this fight, he would once again be an outlaw. He would have to leave Greenland and go somewhere else to live, and he had no idea where that would be. Perhaps he would follow Leif and go west, but would Disa go with him? He somehow doubted it since no one really knew what lay beyond the water. But then what would happen to Disa if he had to leave?

There were too many consequences if he should lose this fight. That being so, he resolved with complete confidence in his abilities that he would not lose.

They pulled into the small island used for such encounters.

Already the holmhring had been prepared. A cloak was secured to the ground, and a series of rings had been carved around it. The final barrier was of rocks set side by side.

He walked across the rocky terrain to the center of the cloak and waited for Egill to join him. Although he had no doubt that he could best the other man, it would be no simple task. Egill was tall and broad, his arms the size of small trees. His dark beard was braided in a single plait that hung to the middle of his chest.

Erik had suggested that he would stand as Thorvald's second. That had pleased Thorvald. There was no other man whom he would be so willing to have at his side.

Three shields were handed to Erik and three handed to Rollo, Egill's brother and second. Then Thorvald and Egill each received a sword. It would be up to Egill to strike the first blow since Thorvald had done the challenging.

Thorvald watched the other man's eyes, for they always revealed a man's thoughts on battle. Egill's eyes moved, betraying for an instant where he would strike. Thorvald raised his shield as the sword swung down. The weapon struck with a resounding blow that shattered the wooden piece in half. Thorvald felt the vibration of the blow all the way up his arm, staggering slightly under its weight. Dropping the pieces, he took the second shield that Erik handed him.

Now it was Thorvald's turn to strike. He glanced at Erik. When Egill followed his look, Thorvald knew his ruse had worked. Immediately, Thorvald thrust his sword forward toward Egill's exposed belly. The man frantically swung his shield around and just managed to place it in the path of Thorvald's sword. The weapon pierced Egill's wooden shield. Twisting his sword, Thorvald locked it into the shield and jerked it from his opponent's grasp.

The other man was startled for a split second; then with a ferocious growl, he reached for the second shield that Rollo quickly handed him. Sword rang against sword as each man fought to defeat the other. In one swift movement, Egill lifted his sword with both hands to bring it down upon Thorvald. Thorvald was already adjusting himself, readying for a hammer blow as before. He spread his feet apart and waited for Egill to strike again.

Egill began moving around the cloak to get a better striking advantage at Thorvald's body. He struck with his sword, and Thorvald met his thrust with his own sword. Over and over, their swords rang out as they clashed together. Thorvald circled with Egill, waiting for his next parry. When it came, Thorvald was able to tuck his shield out of the way against his body and receive the glancing blow without it shattering his shield as before.

Egill's dark look intensified. If Thorvald managed to retain a shield when all three of Egill's were gone, Thorvald would have the decided advantage. It was important not to be the first one to lose blood, for that would prove guilt and end the duel.

Thorvald lunged before Egill had recovered from his own attack. Lifting his sword, Thorvald brought it down on Egill's shield with a slam that splintered the wooden circle into several pieces, barely missing the other man's arm.

Now, Egill only had one shield left, while Thorvald still had two. Sweat broke out on the other man's face. His composure buckled slightly when faced with Thorvald's towering, determined presence.

Recognizing some of Thorvald's tactics, Egill managed a swift counterattack that surprised Thorvald. He went down on one knee, raising his shield to protect his face. Egill's sword sliced through the shield like butter.

Getting quickly to his feet, Thorvald grabbed the final shield that Erik handed him. His blood was coursing through his body in a hot tide, giving him added strength. Seeing victory within his grasp, he gave a cry that widened Egill's eyes with fear.

Lifting his sword, he once again brought it crashing down on Egill's shield. In an instant, the mangled piece lay at the other man's feet. Egill glanced down at the demolished shield, then at Thorvald. There was nothing left for him to do but fight without protection.

Giving his own cry, Egill charged at Thorvald, who quickly sidestepped him. Egill rushed past him and tried desperately to save himself from going beyond the bounds of the cloak. He fell to one knee to keep from going outside the boundary.

Before Egill could recover sufficiently, Thorvald was upon him. Slicing down with his sword, Thorvald managed to draw first blood by nicking Egill's hand. The blood dripped onto the cloak. Erik roared for the fight to cease.

Dragging the air into his lungs, Thorvald dropped his weapon and turned to face Erik. His breathing was coming in short, quick gulps. It was the widening of Erik's eyes that warned Thorvald. He turned, lifting his shield at the last moment.

Egill's sword slammed through his shield, biting into Thorvald's shoulder. Grimacing with the pain, Thorvald twisted to kick Egill's feet out from under him. The man landed on his back with a loud thump, his breath audibly rushing out of him.

Erik's bellow caused Thorvald to stop with his sword raised for a killing blow. He had to force himself to quietness, taking deep, calming breaths.

Erik strode over to the holmgangustadr, his eyes flashing

fire. Rollo was helping a furious Egill to his feet when Erik's wrathful look settled upon them.

"You are a coward, Egill Horiksson!"

Shaken, the brothers stood before Erik with their heads bowed. What Egill had done would dishonor him among those present and, if word spread, among the whole settlement.

Thorvald brushed the sweat off his face with his good shoulder. Erik pointed to his injured shoulder. "You need to have that attended to."

Thorvald had forgotten the injury. He placed his hand over the wound to staunch the flow of blood. If not for his shield, the sword would have left him with permanent injuries to that arm. "I will do so."

Erik looked around at those present. "Thorvald was the first to draw blood, thereby proving his innocence." The other judges nodded agreement. The two brothers bowed their heads before the judges' contemptuous regard.

Rowing back to the mainland, Thorvald could only wonder how Disa would react.

❧

"Sit down, I said!" Disa shoved Thorvald into the bench behind him. His legs buckled against the seat, and he plopped down hard.

Hovering over him, Disa tutted over his bleeding shoulder. Her face paled when she saw the depth of the cut. "But I do not understand. If you drew first blood, how came you to be cut? The fight should have ended with Egill's blood spilling."

She took the basin of water that Agnes handed her and began cleansing the wound. When she glanced up, she found Thorvald watching her intently. Their faces were close together, and the memory of how she had behaved before the holmgang flooded her mind. His kiss still burned on her lips. Coloring hotly at his sly grin, she moved away to get another rag to bind the wound.

"Egill attacked me after the fight had ended," Thorvald explained.

Disa whirled to him in surprise. "What?" She glared at him and felt hot with fury. "I should have known! They are all alike!"

Agnes's voice was like a soothing balm on a festering wound. "Perhaps if they knew the Lord Jesus, they might change."

Disa felt the anger drain from her. Agnes was right, but somehow she didn't have much confidence in that coming to pass.

Disa tied the rag over the wound, standing back to study her work. "It will hurt you for some time," she told Thorvald.

He shrugged. "It will be fine. I have work to do."

When he tried to get up, Disa pushed him back against the seat. "Not tonight. Tonight I will tend the goats and cows."

A stubborn expression settled across his features. "I will do it."

Disa placed herself in front of him, her fists on her hips. "If I have to tie you down, I will do so!"

Thorvald's challenging grin caused her heart to jump slightly. Realizing that she had no hope of outfighting him, she tried another tactic. Leaning close, she smiled at him, making her voice as soft as possible. "Please, Thorvald. Allow me to do this for you."

His eyes widened perceptibly, and his mouth parted slightly. She could see him struggling with his decision. His sudden grin and narrowed eyes told her that he knew what she was up to.

"As you wish," he finally capitulated.

Trying to mask her triumph at having gotten her way, Disa took her cloak from the peg by the door and hurried out before he could change his mind.

❦

Thorvald watched Disa leave with something akin to desperation. Did the woman have any idea what she did to a man when she tried such tricks? His pulse hammered like the stroking of the oars on a warship.

Agnes brought him a drink. Taking the cup from her hand, he smiled his appreciation. Her return smile left him unmoved. Something had happened to him. Only weeks ago he had watched Agnes with a deep appreciation for her beauty. He still marveled over it; but compared to Disa, there was just something lacking to stir his feelings.

He drank the cool water, sighing with content. Settling back against the furs, he allowed his mind to wander once again. Disa had acted exactly as a wife would. He grinned when he remembered her tutting concern. She had hovered over him much like a mother hen would her chicks.

Suddenly frowning, he wondered if that was how she saw him. Surely not. A woman who felt motherly toward a man would not have kissed him the way she had this afternoon. Or would she? Although she had instituted the kiss, he had certainly been the one to finish it. He actually knew very little about women and their thoughts. Did any man?

Disa was an ever-increasing presence in his mind. It was becomingly increasingly difficult to keep his hands off the woman when she came near. It didn't help that he kept thinking of her as his wife.

When she had suggested that he stay last night, he had been ecstatic. But he would not stay when he knew she was still uncertain about her feelings. His honor would not allow him to take advantage of the situation to further his own interests.

He decided that it was time for them to get their feelings out into the open. He wanted her, but in every way, not just physically. Had anyone told him a year ago that he would be married in a year and happy to be so, he would have laughed in their faces. One didn't share outlawry with a woman. Yet that is exactly what had happened. By compelling Disa to marry him, he had forced her to share his exile. Why hadn't he considered that before? Probably because he hadn't wanted to. Regardless of what he had said, being alone had been nothing short of torture.

Agnes stirred the cauldron over the fire, and he watched the flames flickering in a mesmerizing dance beneath the pot.

A creak sounded from above. Thorvald glanced up, then grabbed Agnes by the waist, pulling her back just as the cauldron came loose and pitched to the floor, spilling its steaming contents over the place where Agnes had just stood.

A piece of driftwood caught his foot; and losing his balance, he stumbled back toward the sleeping bench. He only had time to twist his body to take most of the weight before Agnes crashed on top of him.

The breath was knocked from his body. For several seconds, neither one of them moved. When Agnes finally stirred, he tried to roll to the side to move away from her, but his legs were caught in Agnes's twisted dress. He had to push her beneath him to be able to get up. He lifted himself onto his hands, his legs still tangled in her overdress.

"Are you all right?" he questioned anxiously, looking down into her startled brown eyes.

"I am well, but what of your shoulder? Has the wound reopened?"

She reached up a hand to feel the bandage at his shoulder. Thorvald hadn't noticed the pain before now, but the ache in his shoulder told him he needed to get up off his hands.

He flexed the arm slightly. "I do not think so."

When he once again tried to climb off Agnes, his legs

were too wrapped in her clothes to be of assistance. Sighing in exasperation, he lifted himself onto his hands again and grinned down at her.

"This is getting us nowhere."

A bubble of laughter escaped from her lips. Surprised, Thorvald stared at her a moment before the humor of the situation struck him also. He chuckled. In the next instant, they were both laughing. Thorvald didn't hear the door open, but he heard Disa's swift intake of breath. He glanced up in time to see the look of horror on her face before she turned and fled.

Scrambling frantically, he tried to loosen himself so that he could go after her. It took a few precious seconds; and by the time he got out the door, Disa had disappeared.

ten

Disa sat staring out on the calm waters of the fjord. A rock dug into her back, and she shifted to a more comfortable position. Drawing her knees up under her chin, she wrapped her arms around her legs.

The hurt inside was something akin to that feeling of loss she'd experienced when her mother had died. Only in some ways, this was much worse. Her mother had been taken from her, true, but her love had stayed with Disa through the empty days that followed. With Thorvald. . .

She shook her head slightly, gnawing on her bottom lip until she actually drew blood. Had there been any love there in the first place?

She could still see the picture of the two of them laughing together, Thorvald's body pressed close to Agnes's. She closed her eyes against the pain, pressing her fingers against her forehead.

She knew nothing about men, really—only what her mother had taught her, and that hadn't been much. But the one thing she did know was that men were extremely physical. She knew that eventually Thorvald would want a physical relationship, but it hadn't occurred to her that he might betray her. Is that why God said not to deny a husband his rights except for a short time? Surely the one who had created men understood them much better than she did herself.

Was it possible that Thorvald was considering Agnes as a frilla? Although she was no longer a slave, might he still be considering her as his concubine? Surely Agnes would never agree to such a thing, yet didn't the saying go "Better a good man's frilla than married badly." Perhaps Thorvald was regretting the restrictions he had accepted with his marriage and was seeking an outlet elsewhere.

Thorvald had never admitted to loving her, had he? But she had believed it to be so. She had wanted it to be so. Now she realized that her loneliness had driven her to imagine things that had not been.

She remembered his kiss from that morning, and her whole body grew warm. No, a kiss was no indication of love. If a woman threw herself into a man's arms, wouldn't any man take advantage of it? After all, it was the way of men.

At first she had been angry with Agnes, but then she realized that Agnes had said from the beginning that Thorvald was a fine man. Hadn't she suspected that the woman had feelings for him? And hadn't she seen Thorvald watching Agnes?

No, if anyone was to blame, it was Disa herself. Thorvald had honored his promise to her mother, but she could have refused him. If she had, maybe he and Agnes would have had a chance to find happiness together.

Maybe they still could. The thought brought a sharp pain, but it had to be considered. If she stepped aside, Thorvald and Agnes would then be free to find the love she felt certain they shared.

She pulled her cloak more tightly about her. The sun had dropped low, and the air had taken on a chill. Soon it would be dark. She shivered but couldn't bring herself to go back into the house. She could stay outside for the night and return in the morning, even though the night would last but a few hours. Feeling sorry for herself, she wondered if she might freeze to death anyway, and thus free Thorvald and Agnes to marry.

Something cold and wet touched her hand, and she jumped to her feet with a scream. Through the dim light, she was able to see a furry body with gleaming eyes staring up at her. "Knut! How did you get here?"

She knelt and pulled the wolf pup close. He snuggled against her, his tail wagging a joyous rhythm.

Torchlight followed in the pup's wake, and Disa felt her heart hammer with dread. She heard Thorvald's deep sigh when he spotted her.

"I knew the pup would find you," he told her, grinning.

He held the torch forward and examined her face. The silence seemed to magnify his tisk of impatience. She willed herself to calmness, staring steadily back at him.

"Woman, you are enough to try the patience of the gods themselves!"

Disa flinched at the harshness of his voice, her feelings a mixture of annoyance and relief. "Go away, Thorvald."

"I can explain," he told her, placing the torch on the ground and reaching for her. She slapped his hands away.

"Do not touch me!"

She watched the anger spark in his eyes, but he dropped his hands to his sides. "If you would listen to me."

She shook her head. "There is nothing to say. I saw what I saw."

"What you saw—"

"Enough!" Disa snapped. "It does not matter. I was surprised, that is all. You and Agnes may do whatever you wish, but please wait until I am not present."

The flaring of his nostrils was her first warning. Stepping back quickly, she managed to put a short distance between them, but he followed. She continued to back away, and he continued to pursue until finally she could move no farther with the rocky hill behind her.

He didn't touch her, but his hard gaze held her in place as effectively as a snare. "You do not mean that," he stated, the very quietness of his voice giving her a thrill of fear.

Agnes had told her what the Scriptures said about lying, but those warnings had no effect on her for the moment. She was beyond heeding reason.

"I do mean it," she said. "I will divorce you, if you so wish it."

"I do not wish it," he ground out. "I promised your mother that I would take care of you, and take care of you I will or die trying."

He almost shouted those last words. Still, what he had said had not made the situation any better. Honor was a hollow reason for marriage. Perhaps if she had managed to keep better control of her own feelings, it would not have been so bad; but having discovered that she loved him, she now wanted only his happiness. It hurt her to think of giving him up, but her love for both the man and Agnes made Disa regret her hasty marriage.

❧

Thorvald stared hard at Disa. Were she not a woman, he would have struck her, so great was his anger. His first thought had been to find her and explain what she had seen. Now his stubborn pride refused to let him do so. If she could hold such a low view of him, what more was there to say? "Come," he told her coldly, "let us get you home."

Her eyes widened at the tone of his voice. If she had any foolish thoughts about staying here and sulking, she could very well think again. He was having none of it.

She reached down and picked up Knut, cuddling him close against her chest. Thorvald retrieved the torch and motioned her ahead of him. They returned to the house in absolute silence.

Agnes glanced up from her place by the fire when they

walked in. Her face was a study in concern. She got quickly to her feet. "Disa?"

Disa glanced away from her. "I need to see to setting the bread for the morrow."

Thorvald flashed Agnes a warning look, but she hurried after Disa, ignoring his caution.

Picking up his sword from where he had left it by the fire, he headed for the door. "I will be gone for some time," he told them. "Perhaps when I return we can work this out."

Two surprised pairs of eyes met his, but it was Disa who asked, "Where are you going?"

His slight smile held sarcasm. "If I did not know better, I would say that you sound like a concerned wife." When she flushed with color, he relented of his harshness. "I am going on the hunt to Nordsetur. If there is anything that you need done before I leave in two days, let me know."

He crossed to stand before Disa, his cold eyes staring hard into hers. What he wanted to say, he firmly closed his lips against. Reaching forward, he lifted the keys to his house from the chain where they hung pinned to Disa's dress. "You have my keys. If you need anything, use them."

He pointed to the ceiling where the cauldron had once again come loose. "I will fix that tomorrow." He watched Disa guardedly. "Agnes will explain it to you."

Nodding at them both, he left.

❧

From the hill next to her house, Disa watched the men loading their ships in preparation for the annual hunting trip. All the men except those who were infirm would be going, hoping to garner enough furs and skins to make a fortune when the traders came again in the fall.

Disa noticed Thorvald's huge form among the others. A group of men stood around, listening with rapt attention to what he had to say. Disa sighed; he was truly a man to be admired.

Agnes had explained what had transpired two nights ago, but Disa had yet to beg Thorvald's forgiveness. Perhaps in the back of her mind she wondered if her husband and friend were trying to spare her further hurt. She didn't think Agnes would lie to her, but perhaps she was not telling the whole truth, either. Agnes had yet to share her true feelings about Thorvald.

Even more, Thorvald had yet to forgive Disa. She didn't blame him really, but she couldn't bring herself to be the first to beg forgiveness. If there was one thing the Norse had in gargantuan proportions, it was pride.

Thorvald glanced up from where he stood and noticed her standing on the hill. Even though she could not read what was on his face from such a distance, she could feel the power of his magnetism. They stood thus, gazing at each other across the distance until the call to board the vessels. Thorvald turned away and climbed swiftly into the ship.

Disa continued watching until the ships rounded the end of the fjord and disappeared from view. She turned slowly back to the house. It would be a long time before the men would return, and there was still much to do.

Agnes was already stirring the goat's milk in the pot to make more cheese. Disa passed her and began lifting the older cheese from the presses. Taking the rounds of cheese, she coated them with whale oil and salted them. After she sewed the cheeses into sacks, she went and stood beside Agnes. "We will have to get more salt from the traders. We are very low."

Agnes nodded but continued stirring the pot. Although Disa had listened to Agnes's explanation and, to some degree, believed it, it had caused a breach in their relationship that had yet to heal. Disa was sorry that this was so, but she couldn't seem to control herself. For so long she had had no faith in herself as a woman who could attract a man—especially in the company of one so beautiful as Agnes.

Then Disa had allowed herself to care and had been hurt in return. Now she was afraid to emerge from her protective shell. Besides, she still believed that Thorvald and Agnes really had feelings for each other, but that they either were unaware of it or were trying to spare her further hurt.

When Thorvald returned, they would all have to discuss it. If God hated divorce, then Disa would stay married. Still, if Thorvald was thinking of having Agnes as a frilla, she would rather they go and live on his farm. Or else she would. The thought of watching them together didn't bear thinking about.

Disa left Agnes to continue with the cheesemaking and made her way to the summer pastures to check on the goats and their young. Her herd had increased greatly this year, and it would take much more hay to feed them this coming winter. It would probably be necessary to kill many of them and use them for food during the long, cold months ahead, but that would still leave her with a great number to use for wool, cheese, and butter.

She crossed to the hill that led up to Thorvald's house and began the steep climb. She would check to make certain that all was well before returning home.

The hut had an abandoned feel already. Disa dipped a cup of water from the bucket that sat in the kitchen and drank thirstily. Setting the cup on the table, she crossed to where Thorvald kept his keepsake chest. It was locked, of course; and Disa fiddled with the keys that would open it. Did she dare? Thorvald had said if she needed anything, she was allowed to use it; but in this case, she only wanted to satisfy her curiosity. What did that chest contain?

She sat down on the earthen bench that ran along one wall

of his home. She rubbed her hand slowly over the soft white
fur that he must use as a blanket. What did he think about
when he lay here in the night? Did he long for Iceland, or
was he content to be here all alone?

And did he ever think of her? Or were his thoughts on the
beautiful Agnes?

Disgusted with herself, she got quickly to her feet and left,
closing the door tightly behind her.

≈

Thorvald watched the others as they finished claiming their
share of the stranded whale. Each man worked to salvage as
much from the animal as possible.

The hunting had gone well. Now it was time to return
home. The ships were fully loaded with white bear furs,
foxes, seal skins, walrus tusks, musk oxen, and now the
beached whale that had been an added bonus.

Thorvald himself had done extremely well. With all the
furs and skins he had managed to gather, they would be well
supplied when the traders returned. That should be soon.

More than the fact that he had done well, the thought of
returning home pleased him greatly. Would Disa welcome
him or reject him? Had Agnes explained that what she
thought she saw was not what it had seemed?

His anxiety over the whole affair left him in a surly mood.
The others had given him a wide space, and he had not had
to contend with any who would lay claim to what he himself
had trapped or killed. On this particular trip, it would not
have been wise to get in his way.

Erik had planned one more expedition inland just before
they left on the morrow. He had asked Thorvald if he wished
to go with him. At first, Thorvald had thought to decline,
but he knew he would do well to release some of his restless
energy.

They finished with the whale and gathered their weapons for the trek inland. Most would stay in the base camp to guard the ships, but the rest were excited at the prospect of another hunt.

Thorvald followed behind Erik as he trudged up the deep hills that led farther into the interior. Beyond where they were going lay the great ice sheet that stretched for so many miles that it was impossible to see the end of it. The men began to spread out over the area as they passed through, each one intent on finding his own prey.

Thorvald dropped down over a small hill and was instantly out of sight of the others. He stopped to get his breath, marveling over the beauty of the place. He dropped his bow to the ground and pulled out a skin that contained his drinking water.

He took a long draught, allowing the water to dribble down his chin and onto his chest. Brushing the wetness from his face with his sleeve, he took another deep breath of the cold air as the wind blew against his face. The wind was much harsher here than in Brattahlid, biting into a man's skin.

He heard a sound from behind him and turned, expecting to find Erik or one of the others. Instead, a huge, white bear rose on its hind feet to tower over him. Its massive paws raked the air as it tilted its head sideways, its yawning mouth opened to emit a loud roar.

Taken unawares, Thorvald had little time to react. He reached for his bow, but the bear's claws raked against his back, sending him flying to the ground.

Pain seared his back. Gritting his teeth against the burning wound, he rolled onto his back, still trying to reach his bow. In the next instant, the bear was upon him, its claws raking him again and again in its fury.

Thorvald folded his arms across his face, trying to protect

it from the huge teeth that were moving ever closer. His chest, back, and arms were one mass of exploding pain. In that instant when he knew he was going to die, the words that Agnes had shared with Disa and that he had tried so hard not to listen to came to him with clarity. If he died, he would die in sin. He began to frantically pray to be given another chance.

ﾇ

Disa opened the door to Thorvald's house and went inside, leaving the door open behind her. As had been her wont for the past several weeks, she came to make certain all was well.

Of course she also simply wanted to be near Thorvald's home. Being there somehow made him seem much nearer, and she missed him terribly—so much so that she had almost reconciled herself to sharing Thorvald with Agnes. Although it was not something she preferred, it was the way of her people. It never occurred to her that it might be wrong.

She took the cup from the table and dipped herself a drink from the bucket resting there. The cool water slid down her dry throat, and she sighed with relief.

She frowned at the cup, pulling it forward and sniffing it. The water had tasted bitter. She had better empty the bucket and get fresh water.

Suiting the idea to the task, she found the spring that fed Thorvald's land. The icy water froze her fingers as the water ran into the bucket. Disa wriggled them to relieve them of the cold.

She entered the house again, pausing to allow her eyes to adjust to the dim light. She placed the bucket back on the table and went to her usual seat. It was at this time that she would lie back against the furs and imagine her future with Thorvald. In her imaginings, they were always in love and happy. She often prayed to God that it would be so. She wondered if that was a blasphemous thing to do, since it was so selfish.

The interior of the hut darkened, and Disa looked quickly at the figure blocking out the light in the doorway. She got quickly to her feet, the room suddenly spinning around her. She placed a hand to her face, closing her eyes against the dizziness that assailed her.

"Egill! What are you doing here? Why are you not on the hunt with the others?"

His face seemed to move in and out of focus as she tried to concentrate on it. The slow smile that tipped his mouth gave him an evil cast, and Disa shuddered.

"Go away." Her voice sounded slurred. What was happening to her?

"I knew you would come again," Egill stated with satisfaction. "I have been waiting and watching."

Disa blinked at him in confusion. She placed both hands on her forehead, kneading it against the encroaching light-headedness that seemed to be moving in.

He walked to the table and picked up the cup she had used earlier. He turned it slowly in his hands, then grinned at Disa. It was then that she understood.

"You have poisoned me!"

"Not at all," he countered in a smooth voice. "Although I had thought to poison you, my mother suggested an alternate means of getting rid of you. I have simply given you a potion that will bring sleep."

Disa stood swaying, trying to decide if she could escape before he could get to her. Her leaden feet refused to obey her will.

Egill came to her, his eyes moving over her in slow appraisal. His grin was malevolent. When he reached out to touch her,

Disa thought to slap his hand away, but her body would not yield to her commands.

He took her by her forearms and pulled her close against his chest. "When the traders return, I will take you to another fjord and give you over to them as a thrall," he told her softly.

The room swam alarmingly before her eyes. In the next instant, she catapulted into darkness.

eleven

Thorvald opened his eyes to a world of pain. A face bent over him, and he recognized Erik.

"What happened?" Thorvald croaked, dryness causing his tongue to stick to the roof of his mouth.

Erik gave him a relieved smile. "I thought for certain you were on your way to Valhalla."

The heaven of warriors. No, that was not where he had decided to go. He tried to turn his head, but the pain was too much. "Where are we?"

Recognizing his friend's need for water, Erik lifted Thorvald's head slightly and allowed some water to trickle into the injured man's open mouth.

"We are hours away from Brattahlid. We should be there by nightfall."

The water soothed Thorvald's parched throat, and he was able to communicate more freely. "What happened? The bear. . ."

Erik's look was grim. "The gods looked out for you, Thorvald. I heard the noise, and I and some others came to see what it was. Between the four of us, we managed to kill the bear, but not before it had done you great injury."

Thorvald closed his eyes, swallowing hard. He remembered his prayer for a second chance. A prayer to Disa's God. Agnes's God. There was a long pause in his thoughts before he had to admit. His God, too.

"Rest now," Erik commanded softly. "We will be home soon, and that wife of yours can take care of you."

Disa. Would she really? The one thing he had hoped to be able to do if God had allowed him to live was to ask forgiveness of Disa. Not that he had done anything wrong with Agnes. That's not what he needed to ask forgiveness for. No, he needed to ask forgiveness for forcing her into a marriage that she hadn't wanted in the first place.

He began to shiver and realized that he must have the beginnings of a fever. He tried to will himself to remain conscious so that he could speak to Disa as soon as possible, but it was a losing battle. His body succumbed to its need for rest so that it might heal.

ॐ

Disa awoke to stygian darkness. Her head throbbed with excruciating pain, and she moaned softly. It took all of her will to drag her eyes open, so heavy were they. Her mouth was dry and her tongue swollen, causing her to choke when she tried to swallow.

She lay there for some time as the events with Egill passed through her mind in rapid succession. She wondered where she was. Slowly moving her arms, her fingers encountered dry stubble on an earthen floor. She must be in a barn. Most probably at Horik's farm, if Egill could be so foolish.

Was it as dark outside as in this airless hut? She wondered how long she had been there. How long she had been unconscious.

More of her senses were returning. She forced herself to sit up, holding her head against the swaying dizziness.

She heard a key in a lock. A door at the end of the room swung wide, and she had to hold a hand up to shield her eyes from the sudden light that assaulted her. Blinking, she tried to make out the figure that stood blocking the light.

"So, you have awakened."

Disa recognized Greta's voice. The other woman came

scuffling into the barn until she stood over Disa.

"You and Egill will not get away with this," Disa told the widow, her voice husky from dryness. "Thorvald will come looking for me."

Greta threw back her head and cackled. "Ah, the mighty Thorvald." She smiled without mirth. "If he survives the hunt."

A cold vise seemed to clutch at Disa's heart. "What do you mean?" She tried to get to her feet. Clinging to the earthen wall, she finally made it. "What have you planned against Thorvald?"

Greta shrugged, her smile more evil than before. "There are always accidents on the hunt. It can be a very dangerous activity."

Disa tried to reach the woman, but she staggered forward on unsteady feet. Greta stepped aside, laughing at her.

The smile left the old woman's face as suddenly as it had come. "That land should be mine," she hissed, "and I will have it."

"You are mad," Disa choked.

Greta smiled again. "Mad am I? We shall see."

She turned and swept out of the small building, closing Disa into darkness once again. A small sob escaped from Disa's throat. What could she do? She was no longer concerned for herself. She had to get out of here and reach Thorvald.

She tried the door, but it was locked firmly from the outside. Her legs began to shake with weakness. Leaning against the portal, she allowed herself to slide down its length until she was once again resting on the ground. She leaned her head against the door, and tears threatened to destroy her composure. Sniffing them back, she moaned softly. "Oh, Thorvald! Thorvald!"

❧

Thorvald awakened as he was being lifted from the ship into the waiting hands of those on the shore. He flinched as his aching body was jostled from one man to another. They finally made a litter for him using a blanket, and four men carried him up to Erik's house.

Thjohilde met them at the door, her eyes opening wide in alarm. "What happened?" she asked.

Erik motioned for the men to place Thorvald on one of the sleeping benches. "A bear attacked him."

Thjohilde came and started removing the bandages that the men had used to cover the injuries. She gasped at the sight. "Get me my medicine bag," she commanded softly, and Erik hastened to obey.

She worked on Thorvald for some time, and he was dimly aware of her deep concern. He figured he must be in pretty bad shape to cause such worry lines to crease her brow. Again he petitioned the Lord to let him live long enough to apologize to Disa.

Erik left the house to help unload the ships. Before he left, he assured Thorvald that his share of the wealth would be taken to his house.

Thjohilde hovered over him, reminding him of Disa's concern for his wounded shoulder. He needed to see her, and he needed to do so now.

When he tried to rise, Thjohilde pushed him back against the furs. "Just where do you think you are going?"

"I need to go home," he told her weakly.

She smiled slyly. "I know you are anxious to see your wife, but that will have to wait. I have sent one of my thralls to fetch her. You will not be going anywhere for awhile."

Sighing, he settled back, waiting for Disa to come. Incoherent thoughts jumbled through his head, and he could not find the words he wanted to say.

It was a long time before Thorvald heard a knock at Thjohilde's door. He felt his heart start to pound in expectation, his mouth suddenly going dry.

Thjohilde moved to open the door, far too slowly for Thorvald's peace of mind. She threw back the door, and Thorvald heard the surprise in her voice. "Come in."

Disa did not come into the room. Instead, a very distraught Agnes hurried over to Thorvald, her quick look taking in his condition. "Thorvald."

Her face contained a curious mixture of emotions. The only one that concerned Thorvald was the evident anxiety.

"Where is Disa?"

Agnes glanced quickly at Thjohilde, who was listening unabashedly to their conversation. She turned back to Thorvald, and he noticed how pale she was. She had thinned considerably in the weeks he had been gone. Something was obviously distressing her.

"Disa is gone. I cannot find her."

Fear sliced through Thorvald. He tried to rise, but his body wouldn't let him. Growling, he told Agnes, "Help me up."

Thjohilde pushed Agnes away very firmly. "She will do no such thing." Placing a hand on his chest, she kept him firmly in place. "You will stay just as you are if you want to live."

Agnes was gently gnawing her lower lip, her hands twisting and untwisting in her distress. "I have looked for her everywhere. I can find no sign of her. She went to your house, and she never returned. When I went to find her, the door was open and Disa was gone."

Thjohilde looked at her in surprise. "How long ago was this?"

Agnes glanced quickly at Thorvald, then back to Thjohilde. "It has been almost two days."

"Days?" Thorvald once again tried to rise and was again

held in check, not only by Thjohilde, but also by the weakness that was once more stirring through his body.

He gritted his teeth against this fresh onslaught of pain. He had to go and find Disa. If anything happened to her, he didn't know what he would do.

"Why did you not come to us sooner?" Thjohilde asked Agnes.

Agnes ducked her head, and Thorvald knew that she was trying to spare Disa and him embarrassment. Obviously, the girl thought that Disa had left him.

"No matter," Thorvald interrupted. "I need to go and find her."

Thjohilde shook her head. "You are in no condition to do so, Thorvald. We will see what Erik says when he returns from unloading the ships."

Thorvald had to be content with that.

Agnes gingerly seated herself next to him on the bench. "What can I do?" she asked Thjohilde.

Thjohilde handed her a steaming cup. "See that he drinks this. It will help stave off the infection."

While Agnes helped Thorvald to drink the brew, Thjohilde began preparing a poultice to place on the welts left by the bear's claws. Agnes flinched when she saw the angry tears to his skin.

"It is not as bad as it seems," he tried to reassure her. She looked at him doubtfully, and Thorvald had to steel himself against the thought that he might be much worse off than he believed. He had to get well so that he could go and find Disa.

Erik returned, and Thjohilde apprized him of the situation. He came over to where Thorvald lay watching him. "I will go and see what I can find out."

Thorvald thanked him, relieved that someone was doing something.

Both Thjohilde and Agnes applied the poultices to Thorvald's chest, arms, and back. He drew in a quick breath when the wounds began to sting, perspiration wetting his face. Before long, the pain eased; and although he tried not to, he found himself lethargically drifting in and out of consciousness.

Agnes placed a wet rag on his forehead, exchanging it periodically for a fresh, cooler one. Thorvald heard their voices from seemingly far away. "Some infection has already set in, but if we can keep the fever down, he has a chance to survive."

Agnes's soft voice answered, her tone adamant. "He will survive. He has to find Disa, and he will not rest until she is found."

Thorvald felt warmed by the girl's faith in him. She was right of course. He would survive; and if he had to scour every inch of this land, he would find her.

The voices faded, and with them, his consciousness.

≈

Disa scraped at the earthen walls with a small stick that she had found in the darkness. Although there was little hope that she would succeed, she had to do something. She could not just sit by and let something happen to Thorvald.

The small hole continued to grow as the hours passed, but it didn't take Disa long to realize that the walls were several feet thick, just like at her own farm. Sighing with discouragement, she leaned back against the wall, willing herself not to cry. Tears would accomplish nothing.

She heard the key in the lock and prepared herself for the barrage of light that would follow the opening of the door. Instead, the yawning crevice displayed only more darkness. Night had fallen.

Egill came in with a small torch. He placed it in a slot in the wall, keeping a wary eye on Disa. He walked toward her, and she scooted back on her hands and feet. He stopped, grinning at her. He was the kind of man who would take great pleasure in inflicting injuries on others, much as his father had.

He knelt before her, holding out a plate of food. Disa shook her head. "I do not wish anything."

His slow smile tightened her stomach. "It is safe. There are no potions in it."

Disa didn't believe him. When he handed her the plate once more, she shook her head again. Anger darkened his eyes.

"Have it your way," he snarled, throwing the plate against the wall beside her.

Disa ducked out of its way, giving a small cry of alarm. He laughed, and Disa decided right there and then that she would never cry out in his presence again. She glared at him in impotent rage. "Who really killed your father, Egill?"

Where the words had come from, she had no idea, but they had a devastating effect on Egill. He got quickly to his feet, glaring at her in anger. Yet fear lurked behind the anger.

"Thorvald did," he spat out.

She shook her head slowly from side to side. "You know that is not true. Whoever killed your father might just as well kill you."

He stepped toward her, his hands clenching into fists at his sides. When Disa stared him down, he stopped, towering over her.

"Get up!" he commanded, and Disa knew it would be wise to obey. She got to her feet.

He gripped her arm so hard that she almost cried out in pain, but she bit down hard on her lower lip to keep from doing so.

He jerked her out the door and marched her over to the farm's longhouse. Opening the door, he shoved her roughly inside.

Two oil lamps gave very little light to the smoky interior. Filth and grime were everywhere, and Disa shivered with distaste.

With a sweeping gesture, Egill brushed old bones and food from the table in the center of the room. He dropped a load of fish on its surface.

"You might as well make yourself useful while you are here," he told her. "Prepare the fish."

Disa would have resisted him, except she realized that she had a better chance of getting away if she was out of the locked barn. She gingerly sat on a dirty fur and pulled one of the fish toward her. She glanced up at Egill. "I will need a knife."

Pulling his knife from its sheath, he hefted it in his hands. Without warning, he flung the knife. It landed point down in the table between Disa's outstretched fingers. It took every ounce of self-control she possessed to keep from jerking her hand away. He smiled at her with approbation. "I begin to see more and more why Thorvald is attracted to you."

Disa didn't like the look on his face. She pulled the knife from the table and met Egill's fierce glare.

"Do not even think about it," he told her softly, a very real threat in his voice.

Taking a deep breath, she began gutting the fish. The task brought home to her just how much Thorvald did for her around the farm. Although she and Agnes prepared the food for curing, Thorvald had always gutted and cleaned the fish. Once again she had to choke down the tears threatening release. "What have you done to Thorvald?"

He leaned back against the wall opposite her, crossing his brawny arms over his chest. "I have done nothing to Thorvald. I have been here all this time. As a dutiful son, I left it to my brothers to go on the hunt while I took care of the farm."

Disa held back her snort of disbelief, but just barely.

"I have no idea what my brothers have planned," he continued, "but I have no doubt they will succeed."

There was no way that Disa could get to Thorvald in time to warn him. All she could do was pray, and she began to do that unceasingly.

She heard Egill move and looked up in time to see him coming toward her. Panicked, she considered skewering him with his own knife. He reached out his hand for the weapon, his eyes daring her to try something. She remembered hearing about a time when Egill had been wounded in battle but had kept fighting even with an arrow in his back. She glanced down at the knife and realized it was a rather puny weapon against such a man.

She placed the knife in his palm. Laughing, he sheathed it quickly. Disa found it hard not to look at him. His eyes glittered back at her, and he quickly pulled her to her feet.

She pushed her arms against his chest. "Let me go!"

Instead, he pulled her closer, his lips curled into a leer. "You could be my frilla," he suggested, and Disa almost gagged at the idea of being this man's concubine.

"Never!" she spat. "I would die first."

His face darkened in anger. "We shall see."

When he tried to kiss her, she turned her head away. She struggled against him, knowing that her strength was no match for his.

The door opened behind him, and Greta screeched at him to let Disa go. He quickly complied, and Disa realized that this hulking giant was afraid of his mother.

Disa brushed shaking hands down her skirt to straighten her dress. Greta glared from one to the other.

"Go outside," she commanded. Egill threw Disa a surly glare and stalked past her to the door.

Greta turned back to Disa, madness shining out of her eyes. "Do not think to turn my son against me," she warned ominously.

Appalled at the woman's fey reasoning, Disa hastily assured her, "I had no intention of doing such."

Greta went into the kitchen area and pulled a knife from a bowl. She came back and handed it to Disa.

"Finish what you were doing."

Disa seated herself once again at the table and drew the knife toward her. She began filleting the fish expertly as her mother had taught her. "If you let me go, you can have the land."

Greta threw back her head and cackled. "Oh, I am certain!" She sat down across from Disa. "But I will have the land anyway, so why should I let you go when I could get a good price for you from the merchants?"

"I am a free woman! They would never agree to such."

The old woman's eyes met hers, and Disa was struck by the certain knowledge that the woman was truly insane.

"And how will you tell them when you will be asleep?"

Disa's body suddenly turned to ice. She had to get away from this madwoman somehow.

The door opened again, and Egill peeked his head inside. "Rollo and Geiter have returned."

The two men followed Egill inside. Both stared at Disa in surprise.

"What is she doing here?" Rollo was the first to ask.

"Never mind that," their mother told them. "What of Thorvald?"

Geiter laughed. "We had no need to do anything. Thorvald was attacked by a white bear, and they do not expect him to live the night."

The knife fell from Disa's suddenly nerveless fingers and clattered to the table.

twelve

Thorvald continued to fight for his life. In his delirium, he only knew one thing: Disa needed him.

Agnes stayed with Thjohilde and attended to Thorvald daily, while Thjohilde sent some of her thralls to care for Disa's farm. Agnes's lips moved often in silent petition to her unseen God. Thjohilde asked Agnes about it one day, and Agnes was quick to share her faith.

Thjohilde often shook her head at the Englishwoman's mutterings, but she just as often came and sat beside her, and they would talk about Agnes's God.

Thorvald often woke to find the two women deep in conversation. He watched them, realizing that Agnes had something that the older woman was searching for. Hadn't he felt much the same way himself? He yearned for something to fill the emptiness deep inside that had been with him most of his life. In part, Disa had filled that need. He hadn't realized it until just lately. But even so, part of the emptiness remained.

He remembered back to when the priests had first come to Norway and the other Danish provinces. The men had not been as quick to accept the priests' peaceful, loving God. To them, Valhalla, with its lifetime of fighting and drinking, was far superior to the peaceful, quiet realms of heaven, although Thorvald himself had never desired to go where he would be hacked to death and rejuvenated simply to do so all over again for eternity.

In contrast to the men, the women of Norway had been

drawn to this heaven the priests described as a place without tears where the sun always shone. They held this heaven high in their favor.

Now Agnes was sharing the same truths with Thjohilde. As Thorvald watched, it seemed Erik's wife was receptive to what Agnes had to say, though she didn't commit herself one way or the other. Then the fever took hold once again, and Thorvald's mind drifted away.

Meanwhile, Erik and his sons searched the vicinity, trying to find some sign of Disa; but their efforts were futile. Thorvald grew more restless as time passed, but his mind was too foggy from fever to comprehend clearly all that was happening around him.

One morning, he woke clearheaded and alert for the first time in days. Agnes stopped by to check on him and found him wide awake. She reached forth a hand and laid it on his brow, smiling when she felt no heat.

"You are free of the fever," she told him ecstatically.

He stared beyond her, his eyes searching the house. "Where are we? Where is Disa?"

The smile fell from Agnes's face. "You do not remember?"

Thorvald's brow creased into a frown. "Remember what? I only remember being attacked by a bear."

Agnes seated herself on the stool next to him. Her dark eyes were serious. "When they brought you home from the hunt, you already had a fever. That is probably why you do not remember."

Growing agitated, he stirred restlessly. He rubbed a hand over the bandages on his chest, noting the red welts peeking from the corners. "Remember what? Where is Disa?" He glanced around the room, then quickly back at Agnes. "We are at Brattahlid!"

Agnes nodded. "Yes. You were too injured to be moved to

our farm. Thjohilde and I have been tending you. You have been ill with fever for several days."

Thorvald's eyes narrowed. Why wasn't his wife here to tend him? She had told him in no uncertain terms that he was welcome to Agnes. Had she then decided to remain at home and allow Agnes free rein? His lips tightened. If Disa thought he would allow her to divorce him, she could very well think again. As he had told her, he didn't give up easily what he considered to be his.

He started to rise, and Agnes grew alarmed. She placed a hand against his chest, trying to keep him in place. "What are you doing?"

Although her strength was no match for his when he was in a fit state, she was more than a match for him in this weakened state. He relaxed back against the bed.

"I need to talk to Disa."

The distress on her face did nothing to alleviate his anxiety. "Thorvald, Disa has disappeared. Erik and his men have been trying to find her, but they have not had any success."

At that moment, Thorvald could have wished for some of the heat from his fever to return because his body suddenly felt like ice. For several seconds, he could not think. "What do you mean, she has disappeared? Where could she have gone?"

"I do not know. One day she went to check on your house, and she never came back."

Filled with dread, Thorvald shoved her hand from his chest and tried to sit up. He had to grab his head as the world tilted crazily around him.

Agnes placed a hand on his arm. "Thorvald, there is nothing that you can do right now. Erik and the others are searching the area. He has even sent runners to the other farms to see if anyone knows anything."

Frustrated with his weakness, Thorvald growled low in his

throat. The will might be there, but his body was not going to allow him to do what he knew he must.

He was helpless when both Agnes and Thjohilde pushed him back against the furs again.

"Erik will keep looking, Thorvald," Thjohilde assured him. "Surely someone must know something. She would not just disappear."

Agnes pulled a fur up to cover his chest and pushed the hair from his eyes. "We will find her, Thorvald. But you must save your strength and get well quickly to do so."

Thorvald pushed his head back against the cushions, closing his eyes. She was right. He must concentrate on healing as quickly as possible. The longer it took, the less chance Disa had of being found.

He pulled his thoughts up short. No, he would not think that way. Surely she was just paying him back for the injury she supposed that he had done to her. And if that were so, may Thor help the woman.

Thor. No, it was not Thor he should be concerned about. It was not Thor to whom he had prayed for a second chance. Remembering that prayer and its effect, he turned his thoughts once more to Disa's God. *Heal me quickly, I beg You. Wherever she is, keep her safe and help me find her.*

❧

Disa heard the key in the lock again and retreated farther into the darkness. The door opened, and she could not tell who was standing with his back to the light. She assumed it was Egill and tried to scramble back to where the light didn't penetrate.

Instead of Egill, Rollo entered. He peered into the darkness, trying to find her. "I have brought you some food and drink."

Disa didn't move. Rollo came closer, still trying to see in the dim light. "I will not hurt you," he told her softly.

Although his voice sounded sincere, Disa had no reason to believe him. To her way of thinking, his entire family was insane.

Rollo placed the plate of food on the floor, along with the wooden cup of water. He peered through the gloom. "I will leave the food here. You can eat it when you wish."

Disa didn't answer him. He stood for a few minutes; then sighing, he turned and left, closing the door firmly behind him.

Although Disa didn't trust the food, she hadn't eaten in two days. She crawled across the floor in the blackness, careful to move her hand over the ground in front of her.

Her hand finally touched the plate, and she pulled it into her lap. It bothered her to eat with such dirty hands, but that couldn't be helped. She ate the dried fish, swallowing it down with the cup of goat's milk. The food was not very well prepared, but it satisfied her hunger somewhat.

She carefully placed the empty utensils next to the door and once again withdrew to the spot where she had begun digging. The hole was now about a foot deep into the wall. She knew it was probably a useless gesture, but she had to do something to try to escape.

After a time, she rested from her labors. She hated to stop, because then the thoughts flooded her mind. Thoughts of Thorvald. She felt a sob rising in her throat. Was he truly dead? Was it only last night that Geiter had said that Thorvald wouldn't last the night? It seemed more like an eternity.

She would never have the chance to tell Thorvald that she loved him. She would never have the chance to apologize to him for her petty jealousy.

She buried her face in her dirty palms and cried out to God. "Oh, Lord, he can have Agnes as his frilla if only You will let him live. I will not be jealous. I will honor him as Agnes says You desire. Just please, let him live."

How long she sat there praying, she had no idea. Time passed slowly in the dark void. Hours must have passed, because suddenly she heard the key in the lock again, and Rollo appeared with her supper.

His foot knocked against the plate at the door, and he pushed it to the side. Disa couldn't see his face, but she heard the satisfaction in his voice. "You have eaten. That is good."

This time when he entered, he brought a torch with him. He searched with the light until he found her huddling in the corner. Knowing he had the light, Disa had hastily moved to the other side of the barn so that he wouldn't see where she had been digging.

He placed the torch in its holder on the wall and brought her the food. His towering presence did little to reassure her. This time, he waited until she took the plate from his hand. Instead of leaving, he seated himself on the floor across from her. Taken by surprise, Disa stared at him with suspicion. Unlike his brothers, Egill and Geiter, who were dark haired, Rollo had blond hair. His beard was clipped short, also unlike most of the men she knew. His blue eyes showed an intelligence that surprised her.

"My mother is not happy. She has heard that Thorvald survived."

Disa closed her eyes. Praise God!

"I thought this might please you."

Disa opened her eyes and stared at him. What was it that she heard in his voice? He sounded pleased himself. Indeed, he was smiling. The smile made him quite handsome, and Disa wondered all the more about him.

He turned away from her steady regard and began scraping at the dirt floor with his fingernail. "The woman, Agnes, who lives with you. . ."

Disa's eyes widened, but she kept her silence. It terrified

her that this man had even noticed Agnes. There was no telling what these people had in mind for her friend. Disa would have to do all in her power to protect her. Somehow, she must find a way.

Rollo looked at her again. He opened his mouth to speak, then closed it again. Finally, he found the words he wanted to say. "Does she have a man?"

Disa wondered if she would be lying if she told the man yes. In a way, wasn't it true? In Disa's mind at least, Agnes had Thorvald. But what if that gave Rollo the incentive to seek Thorvald's death? She finally decided to say the truth. "I do not know."

He frowned at her. "How can you not know? You live with her."

Disa wet her dry lips with her tongue. She couldn't bring herself to look him in the eye. "There are some who have shown interest, but Agnes has not spoken of her feelings on the matter."

His face darkened. "What others?"

Realizing her mistake, Disa was quick to assure him. "I do not know their names. They were at the Althing."

The frown returned to his face. Disa had a sudden idea. "Agnes is searching for a man who shares her God."

Rollo looked at her quickly, his eyes sparking with interest. "Which god is that? Odin? Thor?"

"No," Disa answered softly, "it is the Christian God, the One who is the only true God."

He stared at her as though she had lost her mind. "That God is a weak God. No man would accept Him!"

Although Disa had begun this conversation as a way to sidetrack Rollo from his interest in Agnes, she now felt compelled to share her own faith as well. She leaned forward and told him earnestly, "That is not so. Many of our people have accepted Him as the one true God. Did you not hear how He protected Agnes?"

He shook his head slowly, his expression one of doubt. Without realizing she was doing so, Disa scooted closer to him and began telling him Agnes's story. He sat enthralled. It was the way of her people, to share their lives through storytelling. It probably never occurred to him to doubt her word on the matter.

A shout from the house brought both of their heads snapping around. Rollo got quickly to his feet, glancing at the doorway anxiously. "I would like to hear more of this God."

Surprised, Disa could only marvel at God's ways. "I would be glad to share with you what I know, but Agnes knows far more than I."

He looked back at her then, his face softened with feeling. "She must be some woman." He picked up the empty plate from beside the door, and taking the torch, he quickly left. Somehow, the sound of the key turning in the lock no longer seemed so ominous.

❧

As the days passed, Thorvald felt his strength returning. Though painful, the wounds were healing well. His thoughts, though, were more painful than his injuries. Having to lie and stew on the possibilities before him gave no peace.

Agnes found him one morning standing beside the sleeping couch. She hurried to his side. "What are you about?" she asked indignantly.

He glared at her, carefully rubbing his hands over the tender spots where the bandages still wrapped his bare chest. "I have had enough coddling. I am well enough to leave."

Thjohilde and Erik came into the room after Agnes. Thjohilde stared at him in surprise, but Erik had a knowing look on his face. The two men looked at each other.

"You still have not found her?" Thorvald asked.

Erik shook his head. "No. We have asked around for miles, but no one seems to have seen her."

Thorvald's lips pressed together into a tight line. He looked quickly about the room. "Where is my shirt?"

Erik's smile was touched with humor. "There was not much left of it after the bear was finished with you."

Taking a deep breath, Thorvald nodded. "I should have realized. No matter, I will go home and get another."

Erik crossed the room and lifted the lid on an ornate trunk. He pulled a fur-lined leather vest from its depths and threw it across the room to Thorvald. Catching it easily, Thorvald looked quizzically at his friend.

"For you. You can repay me some other time." Erik's smile broadened. "Right now, I think perhaps you have other things on your mind."

Nodding his appreciation, Thorvald pulled the shirt on, flinching against the pain.

Thjohilde was tisking at him in concern. "It is still too soon for you to be up and around."

Erik threw her a disparaging look. "Woman, he is a man, not a child!"

Shaking her head at the two, she threw up her hands in exasperation. "So be it."

After thanking the two for the use of their home, Thorvald made a quick departure.

Agnes hurried in his wake. "What will you do?"

He strode up the hillside, the fresh, cold air giving strength to his lungs. "I will go to my house and see what I can find out."

Agnes scrambled along in his wake. "I wish to go with you."

"No."

He could hear the annoyance in her voice when she answered him. "You should not be alone. Your injuries—"

"My injuries are fine," he interrupted her. He grinned at her doubtful look. "There is nothing that you can do."

She argued with him all the way to the farm, but there was no swaying him. He finally glared at her in aggravation. "I do not know what happened to Disa. I will not have the same thing happen to you."

Realizing that there was no way to change his mind, she finally capitulated. He left her at Disa's farm and continued on his way to his own house.

He found everything much as he had left it. He searched the house for some clue to Disa's strange disappearance, but the only thing he found was a cup on the floor under the table.

He picked it up, turning it in his hands. If only the thing could talk, he might be able to find out what had happened to his wife.

A strange odor wafted to him on the air, and he wrinkled his nose, glancing around to see where it came from. He could see nothing different about the house.

Finally, his eyes came to rest on the cup. He lifted it to his nose, blowing out through his nostrils when the overpowering scent assailed him. He sniffed again, lightly this time. There was no doubt about it; the smell was coming from the cup. Frowning, he wondered what it could mean.

Thjohilde might be able to help him. It had an herbal smell, and Thjohilde was well versed in the way of herbs.

He closed his door behind him, searching the area around his house. He found small footprints at the back of the house near his spring. Disa's, no doubt. Kneeling, he placed his large hand against the tiny prints, gaining some sense of satisfaction at having just this small nearness to her.

Beside Disa's prints, he also found a much larger set of footprints. A man's.

His blood seemed to turn to ice. Some man had been here. Was it perhaps Erik or one of his sons looking for Disa? It was possible, of course, but a vague premonition told him this was not so. He rose quickly to his feet. He wouldn't find his answers here.

Clenching the cup in his hands, he began a sprint down the hill that soon turned into a slow walk. The effects of being incapacitated so long were beginning to tell on his weakened body. Forcing himself onward, he finally made it to Brattahlid.

Thjohilde answered his knock, her face showing her surprise. "Thorvald. I thought you would be looking for Disa."

"I was," he told her, leaning against the doorpost and panting from his exertion. Recognizing his weakness, she quickly opened the door wider.

"Come in. Sit down. You look like you are about dead on your feet."

He did as she suggested. When she turned to get him a drink, he latched onto her arm in desperation. "I need to speak with Erik."

She studied his face, then nodded. "I will call him."

Erik answered her summons, grumbling as he came in the door. When he saw Thorvald, his eyes widened in surprise. Asking no questions, he came and stood before Thorvald, waiting for him to catch his breath to speak.

"My house," Thorvald panted, "have you or your sons been there recently?"

Erik frowned. "We did not think it necessary since Agnes had already been there and searched. Why?"

Thorvald handed him the cup, one arm wrapped around his chest as the pain from his wounds returned. "I found this and a set of man's footprints."

Erik's eyes widened. Thorvald told him to sniff the cup; and, when he did, he gagged at the smell. He turned to his wife, who was standing nearby. "Do you recognize the smell?"

She took the cup, sniffing carefully. She glanced quickly at Erik. "It is from an herb used to cause sleep."

Despite his earlier weakness, Thorvald was back on his feet in an instant. "You mean someone drugged her?"

Thjohilde nodded. "That is my guess."

Thorvald's breathing grew more ragged as his anger grew. The fury coursing through his veins gave him added strength. "Who would do such a thing? And why?"

"You say it was a man's footprints?" Erik inquired.

Thorvald nodded, and he could see Erik thinking.

"Who, then, did not go with us on the hunt?"

Both men quickly searched their minds for the answer.

"Egill," they chorused in unison.

thirteen

Each time the door to her prison opened, Disa dreaded the thought that Egill might be coming to molest her once again. Rollo put her mind at rest after the second day of his appearances.

"My mother will not allow Egill to come near you. She believes you have put a spell on him to bind him to you."

Disa was appalled at the woman's reasoning but thankful for it nonetheless.

Rollo tried to spend as much time as he could with Disa without raising his mother's suspicions on that score. He was eager to hear any words about the God Agnes loved; and after a time, Disa noticed a softening of his features. He was as unlike his other two brothers as it was possible to be. She wondered how this had come about, thankful that God had seen fit to make it so.

The words Agnes had said before came back to her now. Perhaps if they knew the Lord. Rollo seemed as hungry for God as both Disa and Agnes; and though Disa was nowhere near as knowledgable as Agnes, she was happy to share what she had learned.

One day, Disa got up enough courage to ask a question that had been uppermost in her mind. "Rollo, why did you tell the godar that Thorvald had murdered your father?"

Rollo's face whitened considerably, and he glanced quickly at the partially closed door before lowering his voice to a whisper. "My mother commanded it."

Disa still didn't understand, and she told him so. He shook

his head at her, his blue eyes filled with terror. "You do not understand. My mother would kill me if I went against her."

Disa stared at him in astonishment. "Surely not! A mother would not murder her own child!"

Rollo's laugh was without humor. "You know our people better than that. Fathers and mothers alike murder their children every day!"

Disa remained silent, thinking about what he had just said.

"My mother killed my father," he told her, his voice a hoarse whisper. "She had Egill steal Thorvald's knife when he was not looking." His breathing came in shallow, fearful gasps. "And she would not hesitate to do the same to anyone who stands in her way."

Shivering, Disa studied his fearful countenance and realized that he was truly terrified of his mother. "She is mad!" Disa told him heatedly.

He nodded in agreement. "She is that, but she is also wily above anything or anyone I have ever known. Egill knows that if he follows her, he will one day be a wealthy man."

"Or a dead one," Disa admonished.

Again, Rollo nodded. "That is my fear also." He withdrew into a dark silence, his mind on thoughts that Disa could have no idea of.

"Rollo," Disa said, resting her hand gently on his arm, "you must free yourself from your mother's hold."

His eyes grew more fearful, and he pulled away. "You do not understand. If she does not kill me, Egill or Geiter will."

Disa gnawed her lower lip uneasily. "Perhaps you could go to the godar."

He shook his head solemnly. "The Althing is not for several months. My mother has a long arm. I would never be able to live long enough to make a case against her. And it would be my word against both of my brothers'."

Disa realized that this young man was the only hope she had of escape. If she could convince him to take her and leave. . .

"Thorvald would protect you."

Rollo's smile was sad, and again he shook his head. "They are still not certain if Thorvald will live, and even if he does, he would never be able to fight my brothers in his condition."

"Erik would help," she pressed.

He stopped pulling at the worn threads on his tunic sleeve and looked at her. He seemed to be giving serious thought to what she had just said.

A yell from the house brought him instantly to his feet. "I must go." He walked quickly to the door but hesitated before leaving. "Perhaps you will pray for me," he requested quietly.

"I already have been," she answered just as quietly.

His eyes met hers through the gloom, and for the first time, Disa recognized a spark of hope in his. Nodding his head at her, he ducked outside.

ða

Thorvald slid his sword into its baldric and latched it to his side. Snatching his knife, he shoved it into his belt.

A thunderous rapping at his door sent him quickly to open it. Erik and his son, Thorvald, stood outside, their weapons in evidence. Thorvald stared at them in surprise.

"We have come to go with you."

Thorvald opened his mouth, then closed it firmly. "No. This is something I must do on my own."

Erik folded his arms across his chest. "You are not well enough to battle three men in full health. Besides, it would be better to have witnesses to show that you did not commit murder."

If it turned out that Egill had harmed Disa in any way,

Thorvald thought that witnesses or not, he had just that thing in mind.

Thorvald followed the other two men out the door, closing it behind them. "I must go to Disa's farm first. I intend to bring her pup. If Disa is anywhere in the vicinity, Knut will find her."

Erik nodded, and he and his son fell into step beside Thorvald. Anyone who knew Thorvald at all would see he was more than ready for battle, and Erik knew him well.

Thorvald's smile was without mirth as he turned to Eric.

"I thank you for your concern." Thorvald then nodded at Eric's son, a man of as fine stature as his father. "And yours as well, Thorvald."

Thorvald Eriksson grinned back at him. "I thank you. It is far too peaceful on this Greenland. I welcome some diversion."

Erik threw back his head and laughed, and Thorvald realized that the two men were hoping for a fight. It just as suddenly occurred to him that that was exactly the way he had been feeling himself. He frowned. But that was not the way of Disa's God. He was a God of peace. Thoughts of what Egill might have done to Disa brought the anger flowing through Thorvald in a swift flood tide. No wonder the men of his people did not accept such a God. He nursed his anger as a mother nurses her baby until he felt fully justified in what he was doing. He would find Disa; and so help him, if anything had happened to her, he would kill Egill.

❧

Rain tapped against the roof of Disa's shelter. She was huddled in the middle of the floor trying to stay away from the walls where insects were scurrying to get away from the moisture.

How long had she been here, anyway? Hours had turned into days, days into more than a week. She was fast losing hope for herself, but each day brought her greater hope that

Thorvald had survived. Rollo always assured her of this fact with evident glee. The news was less than reassuring, however, for the only way that he could know was if someone was spying on Thorvald, and she had no doubt who that someone was.

She buried her face in her upraised knees. *Oh, please God, keep Thorvald safe.*

She heard the key in the lock with some surprise. It was not yet time for her evening meal. Rollo opened the door; and instead of closing it partially behind him as he usually did, he left it wide open. "Come. I have to get you out of here."

Disa got to her feet quickly at the urgency of his voice. He reached forward and grabbed her arm, trying to pull her along after him. Disa resisted. "Where are you taking me?"

He glanced at her in exasperation. "I have no idea, but the traders have come, and I must get you away from here before Egill returns to tell Mother."

Disa didn't ask any more questions. She followed him out the door and up the hill behind his house. She stopped suddenly. "This is the opposite way from my farm."

He slid back down the hill to where she was standing and, taking her hand, began pulling her along. Disa had no hope of thwarting him; he was far too strong.

"I know," he told her, his breathing labored, "but Egill will be coming from that direction. We have to go somewhere and hide until later. Then we will try for Erik's farm."

What he said made sense. Disa followed him, her prayers intensified. She was astounded by Rollo's willingness to help her, but then she supposed she shouldn't have been. Hadn't she seen a softening in him of late as she had shared God's Word? But for it to have so touched his heart that he would go against his mother and brothers, of whom he was so afraid, affected her deeply. Agnes had been right. God's Word did indeed have a changing effect on people's lives.

They scrambled along, going farther from Greta's farm until at last the sight of it disappeared from view. The rain continued to pour, drenching them both in a short time.

After some time, Rollo finally stopped to allow Disa to rest. She sat down on a boulder and looked up at him curiously, her teeth chattering. She brushed the trickling wetness from her face. "How did you know that the traders had come?"

His eyes met hers briefly. "I have been watching for them."

Disa didn't know what to say. Her throat was clogged with tears in a mixture of profound relief and happiness. She finally managed to croak out two words. "Thank you."

He glanced at her again, a slight smile tipping his mouth. He shrugged, but Disa read the fear in his eyes. She suddenly grew frightened herself. If Egill found them, she would be given to the traders, and Egill would most probably kill his brother. The thought brought her to her feet. "I have rested enough. Let us go on."

He didn't argue. Disa followed after him, more frightened than ever.

❧

Halfway to Disa's farm, Thorvald heard the horn announcing the arrival of a ship. He and his two companions stopped and looked out over the fjord. A graceful knarr slid quietly through the calm waters.

"Bjorn has returned," Erik stated. He waited several moments, watching the ship as it came closer. Finally, he turned to his son. "Go to Brattahlid and have your mother invite Bjorn to stay with us. I will continue on with Thorvald."

Thorvald Eriksson seemed ready to argue but held his tongue. There was no gainsaying his father's authority. Reluctantly, he took leave of them.

Thorvald and Erik continued on to Disa's farm through a driving rain that had started some time ago. Agnes glanced up from her seat near the fire when Thorvald opened the door and walked inside. She came instantly to her feet.

"I am going for Disa. I need the pup."

It took her a moment to understand his meaning. A quick smile spread across her face.

"Of course! Knut will find her."

She got the walrus-hide rope that Disa had used when taking the animal with her long distances and tied it around the pup's neck. His tail thumped in appreciation as he stared up at her with panting tongue hanging from his mouth in what seemed to be a huge smile. She grinned back at him. "All right. Go with Thorvald."

Before Thorvald could exit the house, Agnes's soft voice calling his name stopped him. He turned back to her, his wet hair and clothes plastered against his body, one brow lifted in question.

"Please, Thorvald. Mind that you do not bring the sin of murder upon yourself."

Her words once again brought the doubt to his mind. "I will not kill if it can be avoided," he finally told her, uncertain whether he would be able to keep his word.

⁂

Darkness rushed toward the land much earlier than months before. With it came the colder temperatures. Although the rain had finally stopped, it had dropped the temperatures even lower. Since Disa had no cloak to warm her, she huddled against the chilly air. Her teeth chattered as she rubbed at her arms briskly, trying to bring some warmth to her freezing body. Rollo seemed unaffected. He was watching the area behind them for signs that they were being followed. His edginess communicated itself to Disa, making her more anxious by the minute.

She saw Rollo tense. "Someone is coming."

Disa got to her feet, ready to flee. She had no idea in which direction to go, but she would not stay to be caught like a seal in a trap.

Rollo drew his sword, his jaws clenched tightly in expectation of the battle to come. He released his breath in sudden surprise. "It is a wolf pup!"

Disa scrambled hastily over the rocks just in time to see Knut pull himself over the ledge. Her eyes widened in surprise.

"Knut! How—"

Thorvald appeared on the hill. His eyes went from Disa cuddling the pup to Rollo standing with his sword drawn. Too surprised to move or speak, Disa and Rollo stood still as Thorvald slowly drew his sword from its baldric. His eyes glittered with fury.

Realizing his intent, Disa threw herself forward between the two men.

"No, Thorvald! It is not what it seems. Rollo was helping me."

Both men stood tensed for battle. Disa stepped close to Thorvald. He glanced down at her suspiciously but quickly returned his look to the other man.

Disa shared with him how Rollo had helped her and kept her from harm. She told him Greta's plans for her, and his eyes darkened until they shone black. Desperate to turn his thoughts from vengeance, Disa asked, "How did you know where to look for us?"

"Erik and I went to Greta's farm." A slight smile touched his lips. "I believe Greta was as surprised to find you gone as I was. I was certain that that was where you would be, unless. . ."

He didn't finish the statement, but then he didn't need to. Disa knew what he was thinking. Unless they had already killed you.

Disa saw him visibly shake himself; then replacing his sword in its baldric, he reached out, pulling her roughly into his arms. He buried his face in her neck. "Disa, Disa!"

For the first time, Disa understood the depths of his caring for her. She wrapped her arms around his waist but pulled back at his sharp intake of breath. Remembering that he had been injured, she tried to pull away, but he only held her closer.

"No, I am not yet willing to let you go."

Rollo choked on a laugh, turning away to give them some privacy. He allowed them several long moments before he asked the question Disa had been dreading. "What of my mother and brothers?"

Thorvald slowly pulled away from Disa. He watched the other man carefully as he told him, "Erik has suggested that they might prefer to leave with the traders."

Rollo was surprised. "And they agreed?"

Thorvald's smile lacked humor. "I believe he gave them no choice."

Rollo retreated into silence. No one would question Erik's authority; and if Greta had insisted on being tried at the Althing, with Erik's word against her, the decision would not have gone in her favor. Rollo lifted his chin proudly. "And what of me?"

Thorvald was some time answering. He looked first at Disa, who was holding her breath awaiting his answer.

"I would say that you have a farm to run."

Rollo's mouth dropped open in surprise. His eyes lit like the winter sky when the shining lights danced across its surface. He nodded his head. "I think I must explain to Erik." He smiled at Disa. "I will see you later."

Disa reached out to stop him. "Will you please stop by my farm and reassure Agnes that Thorvald and I are all right?"

Rollo glanced quickly at Thorvald, his face coloring brightly. "I will do so."

Thorvald watched him go, a perplexed frown on his face.

"What was that all about?"

Instead of answering him, Disa pulled his face around until he was looking directly at her. "Thorvald, I must know something."

As he gazed into her eyes, his own softened considerably. He placed his large palms against her cheeks. "What is it, my beloved?"

Suddenly, bereft of words, she could only stare at him. "Beloved?"

"You are my beloved," he said softly and would have kissed her, but she pulled back. His eyes narrowed.

"What of Agnes?" she asked, suddenly very unsure of herself.

A frown drew his brows together. "What of her?"

"You. . .she. . ."

Thorvald shook his head, grinning. "I told you once before; you talk too much."

He kissed her with a thoroughness that left no room for doubt in her mind.

"But I thought—"

"I know what you thought," he interrupted, tapping her nose with a finger. "I never should have let you believe that I had feelings for Agnes." His smile increased. "I am afraid, Beloved, that you dented my pride considerably when you told me that Agnes and I could have each other."

Disa couldn't let the matter rest. "Agnes cares for you."

Thorvald sat on a boulder and pulled her onto his lap. "Agnes and I talked. She cares for me, yes, but not in the way that you think. She loves me like a brother, just as I love her as a sister." He looked down at her. "I love no woman as a wife but you, Disa."

Disa felt a thrill run through her body at his words. It was hard to believe the truth of them. "But she was not happy to see us wed."

He nodded, tightening his arms around her. She settled into the warmth of his arms. "You are correct, but she was unhappy because she knew that I was not a believer. She wanted you to be able to share your faith with your husband."

Disa lifted her face to his, warm feelings flooding through her at Agnes's deep caring. She owed the woman a heartfelt apology.

Thorvald glanced down at her, desire evident in his eyes. It was a marvel to Disa that he could care for her so.

"I am a believer, Disa," he told her, "but I am not certain what this God requires of me."

Disa smiled happily up at him, content to lie in his arms. "Then we shall learn together. Although Agnes does not know all of the Scriptures, she knows many of them. The Word of God tells us how to live. Someday maybe we will have His Word written down for us to read like the priests. Would not that be wonderful?"

He smiled, nodding. "Yes, but the wonderful part will be learning them together. I love you, Disa."

She wrapped her arms around his neck, her eyes speaking before any words left her mouth. "And I love you, Thorvald. Now and forever."

Thorvald got to his feet, pulling her up into his arms. She remonstrated with him to put her down, knowing that his injuries must still pain him, but he would have none of it. "It will be dark soon, and winter is coming."

She saw the question in his eyes. "The nights will be long," she whispered. "Let us go home."

A Letter To Our Readers

Dear Reader:

In order that we might better contribute to your reading enjoyment, we would appreciate your taking a few minutes to respond to the following questions. We welcome your comments and read each form and letter we receive. When completed, please return to the following:

Fiction Editor
Heartsong Presents
PO Box 719
Uhrichsville, Ohio 44683

1. Did you enjoy reading *Viking Honor* by Darlene Mindrup?
   ☐ Very much! I would like to see more books by this author!
   ☐ Moderately. I would have enjoyed it more if

   _____

   _____

   _____

2. Are you a member of **Heartsong Presents**? ☐ Yes ☐ No
   If no, where did you purchase this book? _____

   _____

3. How would you rate, on a scale from 1 (poor) to 5 (superior), the cover design? _____

4. On a scale from 1 (poor) to 10 (superior), please rate the following elements.

   ____ Heroine   ____ Plot
   ____ Hero   ____ Inspirational theme
   ____ Setting   ____ Secondary characters

5. These characters were special because?_____

_____

_____

6. How has this book inspired your life?_____

_____

_____

7. What settings would you like to see covered in future **Heartsong Presents** books? _____

_____

_____

8. What are some inspirational themes you would like to see treated in future books? _____

_____

_____

9. Would you be interested in reading other **Heartsong Presents** titles? ❑ Yes ❑ No

10. Please check your age range:

    ❑ Under 18   ❑ 18-24

    ❑ 25-34   ❑ 35-45

    ❑ 46-55   ❑ Over 55

Name_____

Occupation _____

Address _____

City_____ State_____ Zip_____

Minnesota

*I*n 1877, the citizens of Chippewa Falls, Minnesota, are recovering from the devastation of a five-year grasshopper infestation. Throughout the years that follow, countless hardships, trials, and life-threatening dangers will plague the settlers as they struggle for survival amidst the harsh environs and crude conditions of the state's southwest plains. Yet love always prevails.

Historical, paperback, 480 pages, 5 ³/₁₆" x 8"

❤ • ❤ • ❤ • ❤ • ❤ • ❤ • ❤ • ❤ • ❤ • ❤ • ❤ • ❤

❤ • ❤ • ❤ • ❤ • ❤ • ❤ • ❤ • ❤ • ❤ • ❤ • ❤ • ❤